W9-AWC-670

It Happened at a Hanging

Hattie Clark

THE MILLBROOK PRESS
Brookfield, Connecticut

Photograph on p. 158: *Children's Games* by Pieter Bruegel © Erich Lessing/
Art Resource, NY/Kunsthistorisches Museum, Vienna, Austria

Published by The Millbrook Press, Inc.
2 Old New Milford Road
Brookfield, CT 06804

Library of Congress Cataloging-in-Publication Data
Clark, Hattie Mae.
It happened at a hanging / Hattie Clark.
p. cm.
Summary: Sixteen-year-old Jason Becker travels back in time
to Flanders, 1568, where he saves a young girl from hanging, by marrying her
and fighting against the Duke of Alba and his Council of Blood.
ISBN 0-7613-2521-2 (lib. bdg.)
[1. Time travel—Fiction. 2. Flanders—Fiction. 3.
Persecution—Fiction.] I. Title.
PZ7.C5455 It 2003
[Fic]—dc21   2002008141

Yvette LaPierre, series editor

Text copyright © 2003 by Hattie Clark
Printed in the United States of America
All rights reserved
1 3 5 4 2

For Wyn, Keith, and Peter
And for Moo wherever she is

Chapter One

"No way," she said and slid her hand from his grasp. A small pout clouded her face.

Jason said nothing.

"I hate the Art Institute. You know that. There's no way I'm going there again." Karen's words were crisp and final.

Jason let her rant as he opened his bag lunch. He thought she was sexy even when she was angry.

"You think the Art Institute is Chicago's gem. Well, I don't. It's boring." Karen pushed a strand of black hair back into place, then gave Jason's arm a pat. "You can go Saturday morning while I sleep in. And we can go to Saks today, after school. There's a May Day sale."

"Can't." Jason tried to explain that he was in a bind. His assignment for art class was due tomorrow. "It's no big deal. I just have to do a short paper on one of the paintings in the special exhibit."

He reminded Karen that all week long in their free time they had goofed around doing what she wanted to do. He shook his head. " I can't do my research in Saks sportswear. Sorry, honey, I've got to go to the institute right after school."

The buzz and clatter of the Parkman High cafeteria whirled around them while Karen picked over her tossed salad. "You just want to look at the nude paintings," she teased.

Jason sighed. "If I want to look at nudes, I'll buy a *Playboy*, okay? Anyway, there aren't any nudes in this exhibit. The paintings are scenes from the past."

"Well, that should make you happy, all those old pictures. You're so big on history." Her voice softened. "Not me. I like the here and now," she said and blew him a kiss.

Jason wished his insides didn't go all feathery when she did things like that. He wanted to stay ticked off.

"How can you stare so long at one painting? It's . . . It's . . ." Karen hunted for the word.

Jason didn't help her.

"It's freaky," she said. "No wonder I don't like the Art Institute. You're always off in another world."

He shrugged. "The artist froze a moment in time, and I guess I like to think what might have happened in the next moment. And the next. Besides, paintings give you wings. They take you out of here, let you escape to somewhere else."

"Out of here?" Karen furrowed her brow. "Who wants to leave here? Don't be weird, Jason."

She drank her Coke, playing with the straw between sips. Then suddenly she blurted out, "I still don't see why you quit gymnastics."

"That's it, isn't it? That's what's really bugging you, not the Art Institute, not me standing in front of paintings. How long have we been arguing about gymnastics—two weeks?"

Jason had been a strong bet to take first in the all-around for the second year in a row at this May's state gymnastics meet. But two weeks ago, he had quit the team, pulling out of gymnastics completely. Snap, just like that, he did it—because he wanted to spend more time in Parkman High's art studio.

Karen had been furious. She couldn't understand. Neither could Jason's teammates. He hadn't told his parents yet, but they wouldn't welcome the news, either. They liked to see him win, whatever the game.

"You know," said Karen coyly, running her fingers down his cheek, "I'd much rather see you on the bars than messing around with paints and brushes."

For once, her caress failed to warm him. "I want to paint. And draw," he said. "Gymnastics left me no time." Jason also knew he was better at art than at gymnastics.

Anger tinged Karen's cheeks.

Their argument rolled on, round and round like a Ferris wheel, going nowhere, always ending where it started. Halfway through lunch break, Jason rebagged his orange and his peanut butter sandwich. He had lost his appetite.

By the time the first bell rang for class, they were back to quarreling about after-school plans. As usual, Jason gave in. *Maybe we'll go through the park on the way home,* was his consoling thought. He always waited for those moments alone with Karen—in the park and in his Honda.

He sat, watching, while she touched up her lip-gloss and planned their afternoon. She decided that Jason would cut his afternoon classes and go to the Art Institute alone.

"You can be there by two o'clock. That'll give you plenty of time to stand and stare—and turn to stone—or escape to wherever, I don't care." Her voice carried a good dose of sarcasm. "Just be sure and meet me at Rosa's, four-thirty sharp. We'll grab a pizza. And afterward, we can both go to Saks for the sale."

It was settled.

Outside the cafeteria, Karen put her arm around Jason's waist and smiled up at him. Jason liked that. Then she walked down the hall to her English class, swinging her buns just enough to make a couple of guys turn and gawk. Jason left Parkman in a huff.

All the way to the Art Institute, he stomped through the spring rain, shouldering around pedestrians, dodging umbrellas. But when he finally pushed through the institute's revolving doors, his mood brightened. He realized he was exactly where he wanted to be, doing exactly what he wanted to do, and he didn't even care that his jacket was soaked.

He stopped to phone his mom's voice mail, reporting that he wouldn't be home for supper. She probably wouldn't be home, either. Nor his dad. His parents were lawyers who often worked late. They expected Jason to become a lawyer, too, via Harvard. That's why he went to Parkman, one of Chicago's private schools for privileged kids being groomed for the Ivy League. Deep in his gut, Jason didn't give a hoot about Harvard, and he didn't want to be a lawyer. He wanted to be an artist, probably a designer. But when he broached this subject with his parents, they scoffed.

"It's a phase you'll outgrow," his dad always said. Jason didn't think so. Every day he felt his parents pushing, shoving, squeezing him into their lawyer-making mold. He hated it. Whenever his dad tried a big criminal case, Jason had to sit in the courtroom for the summations even if it meant missing school. And whenever his dad made print in the *Chicago Tribune*, Jason had to clip the article and paste it in a scrapbook. Worst of all, his parents introduced him as "Jason, the family's up-and-coming lawyer" as though that were his last name. He dreaded the moment his mom and dad discovered he had secretly applied to the Rhode Island School of Design—along with Harvard, Yale, and Brown, of course.

He hurried to the institute's second floor, making his way to the special exhibit. A hush hung over the galleries. Viewers seemed afraid to laugh or speak in normal tones because they were peeking into someone's past, prying into minds that now slumbered.

Jason searched for the painting he planned to write about. He had seen reproductions of it in art books, and he liked it. It was a busy painting, full of detail, painted in oils on a large wooden panel. In the third gallery, he found it. He read the wall label: "*Children's Games* by Pieter Bruegel, Flemish painter (ca. 1525/1530–1569).

All week long, Jason had used his study periods to read about Bruegel and his work. He had also picked up facts about daily life in the artist's time. Those days were full of fear and darkness for the peasants, frequent subjects for Bruegel's brush.

The exhibit's program shared only a tidbit or two about the painting. It was on loan from the Kunsthistorisches Museum in Vienna, Austria, and it depicted children at play, probably in Flanders, one of the seventeen provinces that made up the Netherlands in Bruegel's day. Dull stuff. Jason had hoped for juicy particulars to weave into his paper. No such luck.

He noticed his jacket had started to dry, but it was wrinkled like corrugated cardboard. Karen would have a fit; she liked him to look neat, all put-together. He ran his fingers over the tan cotton cloth, smoothing it, but the wrinkles popped back.

He settled on the gallery's marble bench and studied the painting. It really was a masterpiece. With his whole being, he savored the sixteenth-century scene that invited him to slip slowly into the world of children at play more than four centuries ago. With no effort at all, he unleashed his mind, letting his thoughts float free to romp with the kids, to roll a hoop and stir mud, to ride piggyback and blow bubbles in the air. He shared the thrill of climbing trees and walking on stilts. And he imagined the giggles of the little girls twirling until their red skirts flared like birds' wings.

Were these kids really happy? he wondered. He didn't see many smiles. At least, their parents weren't pushing them toward a courtroom, and they didn't have to spend a whole evening in Saks Sportswear.

People strolled in and out of the gallery, but Jason noticed no one. Nor did he dwell any longer on his parents or Karen or Parkman High. He tuned every thought to the Brueghel painting.

Eventually, viewers wandered away until Jason sat alone with not even a guard in sight. From somewhere, though, he heard children's voices—chatter and shouts. He couldn't understand their words. *A field trip,* he thought, and wondered why the teacher didn't shush her pupils. He hoped the horde wouldn't invade his space, his "private" gallery.

The children continued to yammer and squabble somewhere out of sight, but gradually their ruckus ceased to disturb him. He focused on the painting, letting it saturate his senses. He could almost smell the briny air of the North Sea sweeping over the Flanders countryside. His nose twitched. And twitched again. He *did* smell salty air. The gallery was seasoned with the tang of the sea.

Bizarre, he thought.

A light wind ruffled his hair. He looked around for a fan or some source of the breeze but found none.

The children's voices grew louder. He glanced around at the other paintings. They were blurry, as though he saw them through rain-stained windows. Only the Bruegel stayed clear. He concentrated on the figures, squat little bodies that played amid light and shadow. He tried to look away again. He couldn't.

He saw nothing except the children playing their games . . . playing their games. . . playing their games. A hoop rolled. A ball bounced. A hand flicked.

Then a mud pie hit him on the cheek. It stung.

Chapter Two

The paintings were gone. So was the gallery. The Art Institute, too.

Where was he?

Fear crawled over him with spidery legs. He had never been so scared. His breath shortened to gasps, and he could feel the sweat of panic trickling down his chest.

He was sitting in mud.

And in front of him, Pieter Bruegel's playground pulsed with life. He saw boys riding piggyback, other boys jousting with sticks, a girl stirring mud. The place teemed with kids. They chattered and shouted and squabbled.

Then abruptly, the kids closest to him stopped their playing and stood bunched together, eyeing him suspiciously. Jason scooted sideways—fast—away from the group, out of the mud onto soggy ground. He scuttled on all fours, crab-style, until his body touched a large tree outside the playground. It was a lone oak in a huge field, and he braced himself against the sturdy trunk.

The kids inched toward him.

He was afraid to think what he was thinking: the impossible had become possible. Somehow he had traveled back in time, erasing more than four hundred years from the calendar, to say nothing of the jump in geography—all the way to Europe. He had been transported to the time and place of the painting.

Frantic, he shook his head, trying to banish the children from sight, the sullen little faces, the squat little bodies. But they remained.

Why had this happened? He remembered sitting on the marble bench and thinking himself into the painting, almost willing himself into it. Well, he'd just think and will himself home again. He closed his eyes, certain that if he concentrated hard enough, this whole outlandish scene would disappear, and he'd be safely back in the gallery. But when he looked again, there was no gallery. He was still in sixteenth-century Flanders.

By now, the children had edged closer. They smelled of sweat and foul breath, and there wasn't a friendly face among them.

Jason scraped the mud from his cheek. Who had thrown it? The girl who'd been stirring the mud? He couldn't tell. They all had dirty fingers. One kid, though, stood out as ringleader, a surly-looking boy in red tights and a gray jacket who lifted a hoop into the air. When he did, two other boys brandished their wooden weapons—not blunt toys but sharply honed sticks, playthings that could serve a purpose beyond fun and games.

Nasty little buggers, Jason thought.

The three boys tensed their bodies, ready to pounce. No wonder. Even sitting, Jason knew he looked big. He was six feet, taller than any of them. His clothes were nothing like theirs. His haircut was strange, and he had appeared out of nowhere.

He knew he needed to do something before all the kids pummeled him with whatever they could wield or throw.

Jason sprang to his feet.

A few of the smaller children jumped back.

With practiced ease, he peeled off three back hand-springs, a handstand, and a cartwheel, tumbling into a split as he splashed a smile across his face, then bowed his head. He had expected laughter or applause or at least a grin or two. But there was no reaction, none at all. The children simply glared.

Finally, a small girl of no more than four broke the silence. Her voice, laced with joy, fanned away the tension. "A tumbler! A tumbler from the fair!"

A wave of relief washed over Jason. He didn't know what language she had spoken, but he understood what she had said.

Almost automatically, he answered in a tongue totally foreign to him until now. "Yes, yes! I'm the greatest of the tumblers. And I'm on my way to the fair." He hoped this explanation might account for his attire of Nikes and jeans and an Eddie Bauer jacket because a tumbler would be expected to perform in costume.

In truth, Jason had no desire to see a Flanders fair. He wanted to go home. But by now, he could no longer hope for an easy way back to the safety of his own century, the cocoon of his former life.

What if he had to live the rest of his days in this place? And die here. He had read enough to know that life expectancy in this century was short. Probably forty, he guessed. Or maybe thirty, what with recurring plagues and persecutions, failing crops and starvation. His command of European history wasn't the best, but he was sure of this: Life in sixteenth-century Flanders didn't roll like his dad's Ferrari. It was mired in muck. Jason pushed down the fear that was rising in him. He'd deal with these kids first, then he'd figure out how to get home.

Small bodies pressed close to him, and Jason felt hands, little and big, tug at his jacket. With shouts of glee, children hung on his arms, urging him toward the fair. At first, Jason balked; then he reconsidered. Life in Chicago had taught him that a peaceful group can quickly turn into a disgruntled gang, and some of these kids were too well armed for him to take a chance.

He forced a laugh, shook them loose, turned a cartwheel, and called, "After you, my friends."

He let them pull him away from the tree, into the mud again, and along the fringe of their playground where trees had already unfurled their new spring leaves.

They hustled him across a bridge that spanned a canal. Its waters flowed slowly along the outskirts of the town, a quaint-looking settlement like a picture in a fairy tale. Outside of town, Jason could see for miles across the flat terrain. It was a spring day with no sun, the sky a great gray bowl overturned on the land. Sheep grazed in grassy fields, and here and there, windmills paddled lazily in the wind. The fair was set up in a field not far from town.

As they approached the fairgrounds, Jason heard harsh shouts and bitter laughter, sounds that stirred his nerves. Once he had been to a state fair in Illinois, and he recalled the tinkly tunes of the merry-go-round and the good-natured babble of vendors selling their cotton candy. No such happy sounds came from this fair.

Would he ever get back to the life he knew? He longed for his parents, for Karen. Especially for Karen.

She was probably waiting for him now at Rosa's. He could almost see her checking her watch, a frown on her face. He wondered how long she'd wait. Until five, maybe. When he didn't show, would she call his parents? Not likely. She'd go on to the sale at Saks, thinking he was still communing with the paintings and had simply lost track of time. The Art Institute would be open until eight tonight, so nobody would miss him for hours. His parents would assume he was with Karen, and Karen would assume he was in the galleries.

When he was finally listed as missing, what then? He envisioned his dad demanding action, his mother dropping every important name she knew, and a cop explaining, "Yes, your son was seen going into the gallery. But after that, well . . . well . . . uhmmm . . ."

No cop in his right mind was going to say, "Poof. He vanished."

Chapter Three

Shrieking, "tumbler, tumbler," the children shoved Jason onto the fairground where he spun into flips and cartwheels and a long walk on his hands. He finished with a flourish and a smile, but the watching peasants stood grim as gravestones.

The bile of panic washed into his mouth when four peasants strode toward him. They had thick bodies and gnarled hands that made Jason think of big Idaho potatoes. As they moved closer, the children backed away.

"Where ya from?" The nearest peasant spoke, his mouth flecked with the foam of ale. He was solid and well muscled from pulling the plow. Even so, a donut of blubber circled his middle where his doublet failed to meet the top of his loose-fitting tights. Jason looked at the man's massive thighs and knew that one kick from this peasant would be crippling.

"I asked ya," the man repeated, "wherebouts ya from? We knows ya don't live in these parts."

Jason's throat tightened. What could he say—that he was from another century, another continent?

"Ireland," he answered, the word rolling off his tongue

after only a second's thought. He figured that Ireland was as far and foreign as the moon to these peasants, who probably knew little beyond their fields and their hovels. "A tumbler from Ireland," he added, feeling reasonably safe with his choice of homeland. "North across the sea."

He watched them chew on his answer. Not a one was ready to admit an ignorance of Ireland.

"Ya be Catholic?" A hopeful tone underscored the peasant's question, and Jason sensed an affirmative reply would be to his advantage.

"Yes." Jason wasn't Catholic, but so what? He was willing to be whatever they wanted him to be. Almost immediately he saw a few shoulders relax and a few grins appear, so he knew his reply had been the right one.

"We wants no more of them others around here, them pea wits that follows Luther and his kind. Heretics, that's what they is. Cause trouble, they do."

Jason stood stone-still while men and women poked with curious fingers at his clothes and his hair. He was well aware that if the men had been more sober, they would have questioned the buttons on his jacket and jeans, the pockets, the cut of his shirt, the style of his shoes; they would have known he was far more foreign than Irish. But marinated in ale, bleary-eyed from carousing, they didn't seem to notice.

Jason breathed easier now that the hostility had cooled, so he wasn't ready for what followed. Strong hands seized him and jostled him back and forth.

"Don't ya know what we do to strangers?" someone roared as ale rained down on Jason in a torrent. More peasants joined the throng, each dumping a mug of ale on him, sluicing it over his head, soaking him to the skin.

"Digna, my girl, hurry it up. Ya knows what we need."

Jason wiped the ale from his eyes and saw a woman waddle toward him, rolling a barrel. Laughter rattled as peasant after peasant thrust a hand into the barrel for a fistful of flour, dusting, showering, and smothering Jason with it until he resembled a snowman in May, one that reeked of ale.

But the game stopped short when the town's church bells began to toll, the doleful notes dropping through the air like dying crows.

Jason listened to the bells and felt the emptiness of despair. If only he were back at Parkman where he knew all the rules. In this place, he didn't understand anything, and he had to give in to others—even to little kids. He looked down at his flour-caked clothes, the symbol of his last surrender. In a far corner of his mind, he admitted that he gave in to Karen, too. But not all the time. And his parents? Well, he had been brought up to defer to their demands. That's just the way it was. Here, it was different. In the past hour he had been pulled, shoved, poked, and quizzed, to say nothing of being the brunt of their stupid game. And he had allowed it all, without even a growl.

The bells tolled on, beckoning to the fair-goers who moved en masse toward a rut-scarred lane. Children clung to their parents or trailed in their wake. Jason followed. Better to join the procession than risk another onslaught of ale and flour—or worse.

Around him people spoke in muffled voices, thick with excitement. Jason tried to make out their conversations but couldn't, except for an isolated word or disjointed phrase. He plodded along with the rest. Down the lane. Around a bend. Carried by the crowd's momentum, he looked only at the rutted ground while his mind journeyed to the twenty-first century. It wasn't until he finally raised his head that Jason realized where he was going.

Before him, a gallows, stark and black, towered in a meadow of green. And beneath it stood two men and a girl.

Chapter Four

No . . . *not a hanging . . . please, no.*

The plea pounded within Jason's brain. He couldn't bear to look at the condemned who waited with nooses about their necks. But he did anyway.

The gruesomeness of the scene exploded inside him, pushing his heart to a frantic beat, greasing his body with sweat. He wheeled about and tried to retreat the way he had come, but the crowd was too packed, too determined in its surge toward the gallows, and he stumbled backward, along with the throng.

Four men, stocky and strong, grabbed Jason and forced him around so that once again he faced the prisoners. He now stood close to the gallows, able to see even the green of the hangman's eyes.

"Ya'll watch like the rest of us," ordered the peasant who still clutched Jason's arm. "When ya sees the hangin', ya'll know not to steal herebouts. That's what they done. They stole." He sneered, showing teeth black with rot. "Ya looks like a stranger bent to trouble. Watch them three, and ya won't take to trouble like they done."

"They stole? They're to die because they stole?" Jason couldn't believe it.

"Don't act like the fool ya looks like." The peasant examined Jason's haircut and his clothes still caked with flour. "Ya don't live here, so ya best learn that's the price ya pay. Them two"—he nodded to the men—"they goes into town and steals a horse. Ya take heed. They's gettin' their due."

The condemned men stood still as museum mummies. Jason couldn't judge their ages, but they weren't old. They were unwashed and shoeless with soiled clothes and unkempt hair. Both kept their eyes trained on the ground. One moved his mouth, possibly in prayer; it was hard to tell.

Jason's gaze then went to the girl. She was a wretched creature, young, maybe thirteen, and she reminded him of an alley cat, scrawny and gray. She wore a filthy garment that hung loose like a long-sleeved nightshirt. Strings of hair strayed from the dirty kerchief bound about her head. She was biting her lip, and Jason guessed she did that to keep from crying. He watched a thin streak of blood course down her chin.

"Caught clean, she was," said the peasant, his grip on Jason tight as a tourniquet. "The little thief was holdin' a bag of guilders. Standing right in the hatmaker's house. None of us out here ever seen her before. None of them in town, neither. When they caught her, she confessed right quick to thievin'."

The girl's eyes stayed wide open, her eyelids seldom blinking. Then Jason realized that she wasn't really looking at the people. Instead, she was staring outward and upward as though concentrating on stars that weren't yet in the sky. He wondered if something somewhere far beyond held her attention, something that kept her from knowing what was about to happen. Not until that moment did Jason fully comprehend the cruel death awaiting the condemned: The gallows had no platform, no trapdoors through which the three would plunge, the fall mercifully breaking their necks. As near as he could tell, they'd be hoisted upward by ropes to slowly strangle.

"Not long and her thievin' days is done," the peasant said, grinning. "Less some no good like yerself aims ta marry her. That'd set her free." The peasant picked his nose and smirked at Jason. "Course that there rule ain't gonna help them men 'cause they's already wedded. We knows that. So they gotta hang."

Jason frowned. "What do you mean?"

"Where ya from, stranger, that ya don't know nothin' 'bout May Day here? Thought that's why ya come ta this town—ta see the special hangin'." He didn't wait for Jason to answer. "Iffen a mate comes forth to marry, the condemned goes free. Not knowin' why. Always been like that at a May Day hangin' 'round here."

The peasant rolled his eyes and let out a loud hoot. "Them old hags gits a chance to claim a mate—iffen he ain't already wedded. And a male that's lustin' gits a queen. 'Course, he gotta wed her, and that's a lump to swallow." With his free hand, the peasant gave Jason a poke in the belly.

How could anyone make light of a hanging? Jason looked around. Everyone stood expectantly, excited as circus-goers in his time waiting for the Big Top's three-ring show. He saw people chattering and giggling, fidgeting and pointing. Some wiggled through the throng to get closer; others stood on tiptoes to see better. All of it disgusted Jason. All of it angered him. But what could he do?

The peasant gestured to the girl. "No prize there," he said as if giving fatherly advice. "Skinny as a bone. Her younguns be dead before they was born. Not much work in them bony limbs of hers, neither. Nobody here so dumb he's gonna risk takin' her to wife. She'd just be another mouth to feed. Best she goes with them two."

Minutes passed before the hangman took his place behind the condemned. The crowd quieted. Jason closed his eyes.

Even without seeing, he knew when the deed was done. For one man. Then the second. No shouts came from the crowd, no screams, no murmurs, merely a collective intake of breath. Once. And again.

When Jason opened his eyes, the twitching hadn't stopped, and he stared, near tears, until death finally settled upon the men.

Now it was the girl's turn.

Chapter Five

"Any takers for this lovely bride—a true queen of the May?" the hangman shouted, his words stained with mockery.

He grasped the girl's chin and jerked her head from side to side, giving a profile view for all to see. He examined her teeth, pinched her buttocks, and fingered two stray strands of dirty hair as though they were golden tresses. "Aahhh," he said.

The crowd roared with laughter.

"Any takers?"

More laughter boomed across the field.

Abruptly, the hangman's game was over. He tightened the noose and with a flex of his muscles made ready to hoist the girl aloft.

"Wait! I'll take her! I'll marry her!"

Jason's offer burst from his mouth before his mind could stop it. Instantly, the consequences of what he'd said struck him full force. But there was no going back now, not with this crowd. They'd tear him to shreds. Already a tumult of jeers and guffaws filled the air.

A half dozen peasants lifted Jason high, then tossed him to the ground like a bale of hay. They rolled him to the gallows and yanked him to his feet.

He faced the girl. At first, he saw only her eyes. They were very large and very gray. He remembered that Karen's eyes were blue. He watched while two women pulled off the girl's kerchief to free a mass of greasy hair, its color hard to determine through the grime. She was even filthier than he'd first realized. Jason saw a flea on her arm, another on her forehead.

Everyone around here has fleas, he thought. *My aunt's farm dog in Indiana always had fleas. Nasty things. I saw my first sunflower on that farm. Why am I thinking all this now?*

A string of crazy thoughts ran through Jason's head: sunflowers and roses and corsages at proms and Karen with blue eyes and blue skies over Chicago. Then, as he looked upward, the thoughts stopped. The sky was getting darker, about to birth a storm. Far off, he heard a cough of thunder, and the spring wind took a restless turn.

The hangman tore the noose from the neck of the condemned girl and untied the rope that bound her wrists. Slowly, the girl wiped the dried blood from her chin, watching while several peasant women started to make a bridal chaplet. The women picked no wildflowers from the soggy meadow for this wedding wreath; instead, they fashioned it from sticks and stems. With exaggerated ceremony, they placed the chaplet on the girl's head, and there it perched like a porcupine.

The girl neither spoke nor moved.

While a piper piped a tune on his bagpipes, an elderly priest, frail and black-robed, hobbled to the front. He motioned for Jason and the girl to stand side by side, their shoulders touching.

A shout cut through the crowd, setting off a chain of echoes: "Where's the dowry?" "The dowry!" "The dowry!"

The girl calmly reached down to the hem of her garment and tore off a strip of dirty cloth. Holding up her hand to silence the crowd, she stepped a few feet from the gallows, stooped, and picked two violets. She wrapped them in the cloth and handed them to Jason. Her dowry.

Jason took the cloth, surprised at the softness of the woolen fabric. Now, everyone stared at him. He wasn't sure why until someone hollered, "The bride price!" and he realized that he, too, must pay something.

Turning his back to the priest and the crowd, he hunched over so no one could see. He pulled a pen and pad from his jacket pocket. His hands trembled; nevertheless, his strokes were deft, and while the crowd hissed in impatience, he sketched a likeness of his bride-to-be with dirty face and big gray eyes and a porcupine on her head.

He turned and gave it to her. For a split second, Jason saw—or thought he saw—amusement touch her face. The crowd surged forward to see, but the priest held up his hands to halt them. No one ventured farther. The girl folded the paper and tucked it into the side of her soft-soled shoe.

Jason now braced himself for the ceremony to come. He had made his decision: He couldn't let her die. He'd never be able to live with himself if he did, and all his days he'd be haunted by the ghost of a girl on a gallows. Saving the men had been beyond his powers. Saving the girl was not. So, he stood stoically as the priest prepared to unite him in marriage with a filthy street urchin whose name he didn't know.

After listening to a jumble of Latin, Jason repeated the priest's words, "I take thee," and then he halted because he was unsure what to say next. The girl didn't tell him her name nor did anyone else. Nobody seemed to care, so why should he? He began again, "I take thee," and inserted, "uhhh, what's-her-name," then continued to follow the priest's lead, "to have and to hold, from this day forward, for better, for worse, for richer, for poorer, in sickness and in health, 'til death us depart, if holy church it will ordain, and thereto I plight thee my troth."

It surprised Jason that the vows were almost like those spoken in the twenty-first century. Hundreds of years had stamped their changes upon the world, yet this pledge had remained essentially the same.

As he choked out his vows, Jason was aware that bodies swung overhead in a wind-tossed dance of the dead.

The girl repeated her vows, but her voice was so low that he couldn't make out a single word.

When the priest asked for a ring, Jason faltered. He'd have to forfeit his class ring. He had planned to give it to Karen. Why on earth hadn't he already given it to her? Not that it made any difference now. He allowed his thoughts to play with what might have been. He might have married Karen, after college, of course. His parents liked that idea. As his mother always said, "Karen is from the right sort"; that is, Karen's parents had money and social status. But besides all that, Karen was beautiful. In his mind, Jason saw her standing beside him. He imagined her in a form-fitting gown with pale roses in her hair. He imagined her smiling. His heart filled with longing.

He pulled off the ring, placed it in his cupped palm and held it out to the priest, who stared at it for a long moment. The ring obviously was not a wedding band and was far too big for the bride. Reluctantly, the priest took it between two fingers as though plucking a cockroach from a holy chalice. He blessed it.

Jason heard his own voice, weak and far off: "With this ring, I thee wed." He closed his eyes and envisioned Karen as he allowed the priest to guide his hand, slipping the ring in turn onto three fingers of the bride's hand and letting it remain on her third finger.

The ceremony was over.

When Jason opened his eyes, his dream of Karen crumbled. Beside him stood reality: an alley cat of a waif with sticks in her hair. His bride.

Chapter Six

The wedding reception—if one could call it that—was straight out of a Hollywood horror flick, the type that Jason might once have enjoyed watching on a big screen with Karen beside him and a bag of popcorn between them. But this was no make-believe scene; he was living every breath of it.

In a rowdy parade, the mob had hustled Jason and the girl back to the fairgrounds. That much had been bearable. The real horror began when the crowd, besotted with ale, sang a stupid little ditty.

> *The thief and the tumbler did wed.*
> *We'll find them a likely bed*
> *In heaven, or hell, who's to say*
> *For the king and queen of the May?*

The words jolted Jason. Was there more to this town's May Day custom than he'd been told? Might they *both* go to the gallows when day was done—dead and dispatched to heaven or hell? Is that what the ditty meant?

He searched the girl's expression for a sense of peace or relief but saw no emotion at all. Then he read the message in her eyes: She was afraid.

By now, the fair's festivities were back in full swing, loud and raucous. A bonfire blazed, torches flared, and no one paid the least heed to a sky darkened by dusk and storm clouds.

Two bullying peasants prodded Jason into the role of servant, and he played his part well, not wishing to anger anyone. He filled mug after mug with ale from an earthenware pitcher, then carried the mugs to the revelers. Here and there, he caught snippets of conversation, soon realizing that people had come from the nearby town and from all over the countryside to eat, drink, and dance, and to sample the fair's special wares of whistles and pottery, brass pots and pewter mortars. Many, though, had come just to see the hangings.

Jason noticed soldiers, too, milling about but never mingling. They wore long red stockings and short bloomers and wide ruffled collars. Their metal hats glistened even in the dullness of dusk, and not a man was without a sword. Fairgoers gave them wide berth, which told Jason the soldiers were probably foreign and not welcome. He stayed out of their way, too, while always keeping the girl in sight.

She still wore the ridiculous wreath and sat in a place of honor at a makeshift trestle table, its top fashioned from a barn door. Couples and singles gathered around nearby tables, gobbling their food and washing it down with ale. Jason's nose rebelled at the pungent smell of pigeons broiling, oxen roasting, and omelettes swimming in lard. He wanted to throw up.

Beyond the cluster of tables, he could see the fair's main thoroughfare where people were buying, selling, arguing, and yelling. The scene was a kaleidoscope of nightmares. Men played tug-of-war, not with rope but with slippery eels. Young couples, barefooted, slid over hard ground made slick with ripe garbage.

Farther on, in a roped-off ring, three blind peasants armed with clubs tried to bludgeon a squealing pig that, so far, had managed to escape any harm. In a lucky move, it wiggled beneath the ropes and raced for cover in the nearby woods. The crowd shrieked, deeming it a joke that the blind continued to club each other, unaware the pig was nowhere near.

Jason cringed and turned away, only to see a bear straining against a chain staked to the ground. Close by, just out of the bear's reach, a woman with glazed eyes and clawlike hands pulled against her own bonds. She was dressed in tatters. *Is she insane?* Jason wondered. He looked away, unable to watch her agony any longer.

His attention went to another woman whose slender fingers fed sticks to a fire. Over it, she toasted waffles to a mellow brown in a handheld waffle iron. A bowl of batter sat at her side. She was extremely thin, but attractively so, and her dark hair was streaked with white. Jason welcomed her measured moves, slow and gentle. Her presence was clearly out of place here where everyone else was rough-and-tumble rowdy.

People feasted, roared, and danced to the tunes of a piper who played until his cheeks puffed into red balloons. Wherever he looked, it was a bawdy brawl. But beneath all the merriment, Jason sensed something else. He sensed fear.

He had read about that fear when he researched Bruegel and his paintings. It was an enormous fear that splintered into a thousand separate fears, each piercing its way deep into the sixteenth-century heart: fear of famine, fear of plague, fear of witches and death, the devil and hell; fear of owls and cats and comets, of moons shaped like crescents and cows that were crippled, and a dozen other ridiculous things that Jason couldn't recall. Today, though, fair-goers covered their fears with fleeting pleasures.

At the moment, Jason had a fear of his own. He was afraid for the girl when he saw two men lift her onto a table top and order her to dance. She shuffled her feet, as though wiping muddy shoes on a doormat, while the rest of her body remained almost motionless. Her eyes were glassy and her arms limp. She looked neither to the right where the bonfire blazed nor to the left where soldiers gathered; instead, she stared ahead without expression.

The carousing rolled on, and as it did, coarse voices with actions to match peeled away any sense of composure that Jason might have held in reserve.

Better to walk blindfolded across a Chicago expressway at night than to be here, he thought.

His nerves frayed further when he remembered the two hanging victims, a reminder that he and she might be king and queen for the night, but then go to the gallows and be dead for a long forever.

The merrymaking was ugly and getting uglier. He watched his bride dance her pathetic dance. He heard the bawdy songs become bawdier, the dirty jokes dirtier.

Then mercifully, lightning ripped across the sky as thunder pounded, and the clouds poured down a torrent of rain. The revelers scattered, huddling beneath trees, hunching beneath table tops.

Jason grabbed the girl's hand and pulled her off the table. "Run!" he yelled and headed for the nearest lane.

But she balked and started the other way, toward the woods where the pig had fled not long before. Jason followed, praying she knew a better avenue of escape.

Across the fields of dank earth, they ran, the cloudburst concealing their flight.

No one followed.

At least, that's what Jason thought.

Chapter Seven

They fled across the field into the shelter of the tower-ing trees and never looked back. Undergrowth tangled beneath their feet, but they pushed on, seeking deeper cover. By the time they stopped to rest, the deluge had ended, and moonbeams once again filtered through the lace of new leaves.

The girl spoke first. "I am Catherine Juliana Eijngaard." Her voice wasn't coarse as Jason had expected but light and airy like the music of wind chimes.

"And I am the daughter of a Beggar," she added proudly.

"That figures," Jason mumbled. He started to laugh.

"I see nothing humorous," she said, her hands on hips that didn't exist. Catherine Juliana had the figure of a twig, and the downpour had done nothing to enhance it. The rain had soaked her dirty shift, plastering it against her body so that every bone and hollow showed.

"Only an imbecile would laugh at a time like this." No longer was there a lilt to Catherine's voice. "Bloody fool! Don't you know we barely escaped death by rope?"

She stopped to let the heat of her words burn. "It was bloody bad, if you ask me," she said. "Bloody bad. We could both have been hanged. Anything can happen these days."

"I'm sorry," he said. Actually, Jason hadn't been laughing about the hanging. It was the wedding that had set off his outburst. *I married a street thief whose father is a beggar. Just the bride my parents would have picked!* he thought. But how could he explain all this to the girl? After all, she didn't know his mom and dad. Nor their demand for the socially proper, their clawing up the economic ladder, their hopes for his marriage to "the right sort." He had smashed his parents' expectations, and it struck him as funny. In a small, odd way it felt rather nice to go against their wishes.

"I'm Jason Becker," he said, extending his hand. It dangled in midair like a dead fish on a line until he finally withdrew it.

The girl said nothing, and Jason could see that her arms remained defiantly on her hips.

"I think we need to straighten out a few things," he said, then faltered. He wasn't good at verbally squirming out of tight spots, not with his parents, not with Karen, and not now, with this girl.

He began again. "Uhhh, I don't quite know how to say this. . . ." He stopped. He started a third time, "I hope you don't consider what happened back there to be a real marriage. It wasn't legal. Anybody could see it wasn't binding. Besides, I'm engaged. Well, not really, but I will be." He wondered if Catherine understood the word *engaged* and quickly changed it to *betrothed*. "I'm betrothed. Well, almost. To a girl back home."

Jason knew he was doing miserably but forged on. "When I saw you were going to hang . . . well . . . I just shouted out. I wasn't thinking. . . . So here we are. What I mean to say is, if we have to be together for a little while, we can act like brother and sister, if you know what I mean. I'm sure you understand." He hoped his blushing didn't show in the moonlight. "I have to go my way and you your way, and I want to go home, and . . ."

"I am indebted to you for my life," she interrupted, her words frosty, "and I thank you. But, my dear young man, I have no intention whatsoever of being married to you, staying with you, or being beholden to you any more than I already am. You also may wish to know that I am totally virtuous." With that, she handed back his ring.

"Good," he said, pushing the ring onto his own finger. "We understand each other. I need to get home."

"Good," she said and took a few more steps into the woods.

"Good," he repeated and stayed where he was. The air around them bristled with tension as when dog meets cat.

"Anyway, it was probably all for naught," she informed him. "They'll find me, and they'll hang me. Or worse." Her prediction was calm and matter-of-fact.

They? he thought. He couldn't imagine those besotted buffoons at the fair mounting a posse to track her. "No," he assured her. "A little time and distance, and you'll be safe."

She shook her head. "They'll find me. Always, the herring hangs by its own gills."

"What?" he said and moved closer so he could hear her better.

"What do you mean 'what'?" she asked.

"What you said about herring."

"The herring hangs by its own gills—everyone must bear the consequences of his own mistakes," she said. "A Flemish proverb."

"Oh," he said and nothing more.

"It's simple," she explained. "I made the mistake of getting caught. And the consequence is that I'll hang."

He was mystified that she thought her mistake was getting caught, not the theft. To him, stealing was the transgression that brought the consequence. *Oh well,* he mused. *Different century, different mores.* He was just glad that he and Karen shared the same code of conduct—most of the time. Karen did sometimes cheat on tests.

Without warning, Catherine Juliana grabbed his arm and pulled him along. "I hear something. There's someone following us."

Oh, no, he thought. *She's not only filthy, she's paranoid.*

"I don't hear anything," he whispered.

"You don't know how to listen. I do."

He listened and heard nothing; he peered through the trees and saw nothing.

The girl grabbed at his sleeve, urging him to hurry. She moved silently. He didn't. Each step he took sounded as though giant beetles were being squished beneath his feet. Jason was painfully aware that he was city bred, out of place not just in century but terrain, too.

They crept along, Catherine constantly looking behind them. "Shhhh," she whispered and placed a forefinger on her lips.

Jason walked as softly as he could.

Suddenly, Catherine broke her silence. "Climb!" she screamed. "Climb!"

Chapter Eight

Catherine shinnied up the trunk of a young oak that was free of lower limbs. Then with a lunge, she grabbed the sturdy branch of an adjacent tree, strong and mature. Up, up, she climbed.

Jason scrambled after her—but had no idea why. For years, his parents and Karen had instilled in him an impulse to obey. Now, true to form, he reacted with a robot's response to the girl's command.

It wasn't until he straddled a branch and hugged the tree's trunk that he took a moment to think: *She's a lunatic. I've married a lunatic. No, I'm not married! But I'm with her. And I'm doing what she says.*

He felt ridiculous and started to climb down. Then he looked below. He counted two, three, no, four forms prowling in the shadows.

Lions and tigers and bears. Or giraffes with short legs. He didn't care what. For the tenth time today, he was scared witless, and he moved back to the branch next to Catherine.

"Wolves?" he asked.

"Where do you live that you don't even know what a wolf looks like?" she said. "They're not wolves. They're mastiffs."

Mastiffs? The word bumped about in Jason's brain, and he wondered if he had seen mastiffs in the zoo and had just forgotten. Animals weren't exactly his specialty.

"Dogs," she said. "They've gone wild."

"Dogs? Those monstrous things are dogs?" Jason was sure each one weighed way over a hundred pounds. He stared down at their stubby faces and the square heads that seemed too big for their bodies. Three snarled, showing vicious teeth. "They'd kill us?"

"Rip us to bits," she said. "They belonged to a nobleman. The tale is that his gamekeeper got drunk one night and just let them out. That was months and months ago. There were more in the pack at the beginning. Hunters have killed a few."

Despite the threat below, the girl sat without holding on, her back against the trunk as though she were cradled on a couch. *How can she do that?* Jason wondered. He had to clutch the tree with both arms.

"Will they go away?" he asked.

"You're asking me? I don't know. I've never been treed by mastiffs before. But I heard they've already mauled two men and a boy."

"Killed them?"

"All three," she said.

Jason found her answer far from comforting.

"You don't know anything about life around here, do you?" The girl shook her head in short, quick movements, and Jason detected distrust in her tone. He didn't answer.

"Mastiffs are usually guard dogs but not these. They were used for sport, bloody sport," she said. "They were trained to kill, and they were thrown into a ring with a bear or bull or boars. The battle was always to the death. Noblemen and clergy find such fights quite entertaining. I find it cruel—and hideous."

Jason's skin crawled at the very thought of staging such fights.

He noticed the girl was shaking and guessed it was from the cold night, not fright. While managing to hold onto a branch, he switched his pens and notepad from the pockets of his jacket to the pockets of his jeans. Then he struggled out of the jacket. "Here," he said.

"No."

"Please," he insisted, and she took it, slipping into its warmth.

Jason heard the rhythm of footfalls as the mastiffs paced below. The little pig from the fair suddenly came to mind. He wondered if it had reached safety somewhere. Probably so if the mastiffs were still hunting for a meal.

The girl's voice broke into his thoughts. "Where *are* you from? This jacket, your clothes. They're from nowhere near." Moonlight played on her fingers as they toyed with the twenty-first-century buttons.

"Far, far away," he answered. "You hungry?"

"Always," she said.

"Look in the pocket."

Her hands fumbled over the jacket. Jason couldn't believe that he was stuck with a girl who had no idea where jacket pockets were placed, but he had to give her credit— she could climb trees like Tarzan's chimp. He leaned cautiously toward her, put his hand in the jacket's left pocket, and brought out his leftover lunch.

"An orange!" she gasped, holding it to her nose, sniffing. "Where did you get it? Papa used to get them. They're so costly."

Jason was about to comment that her father probably never worried about price in his life. Beggars begged, or stole. Instead, he said politely, "Go ahead. Eat."

She devoured the orange first, peel and all, then started on the sandwich. "What's this?" she asked, sampling the peanut butter and jelly on wheat, relishing every bite.

He wasn't about to tackle an explanation of peanut butter. And he was sure that England's notorious Earl of

Sandwich hadn't even invented the sandwich yet. Or been born, for that matter. So, he sidestepped the whole issue with, "Just some ground nuts between slices of bread."

"No one here has food like this. Just where *are* you from, Master Becker?"

Amused, Jason almost laughed at being addressed that way. "I'll tell you sometime—if we live through the night."

"For me, I refuse to hang the cape on the fence," she announced stoically.

"What?"

"Hang the cape on the fence," she repeated. "To quit, to give up."

Jason was getting tired of her smarty Flemish proverbs and couldn't resist saying, "You mean to 'throw in the towel.'"

"What?" Her mouth was full of sandwich.

"Never mind." Talking with her was too difficult. They were centuries apart. He and Karen may have argued, but at least they knew what the other was saying.

"I won't hang the cape on the fence because Papa would never give up. So I mustn't. Anyway, this isn't the way I want to die: in the jaws of mastiffs. By rope or torture, either. I wish very much to grow old and die in my bed, a big bed with a coverlet of feathers."

"And how old is old?" he asked.

"Forty," she answered without hesitation.

"Forty?" A picture of his mom flashed before him. She was past forty—with no gray hair and no wrinkles. And she wouldn't even admit to being middle aged, let alone old.

"How old are you?" he asked.

"Fifteen."

"Fifteen? Really? I thought you were younger."

"Most people do. That's because I'm skinny," she said. "And you?"

"Sixteen." But he had frequently been told that he acted older, maybe because he had skipped a grade and was always with older kids, parroting their actions.

He watched while Catherine finished the sandwich. Her manners surprised him: She ate daintily, taking small bites, chewing with her mouth closed, and never licking her fingers. What amazed him, too, was her speech. It was more refined than he expected from a beggar's daughter. Most of all, he admired her calm. Maybe that was because she had faced death before. He never had.

"What can we do?" he asked.

"Nothing. Wait," she said. "And pray they go away."

"Aren't you afraid?"

"Yes, I'm very afraid," she said. Her voice was sure and steady as though she spoke of mundane things like stirring soup or sweeping floors.

"Well, killer mastiffs are certainly something to be afraid of," he offered.

"I know my fate with them," she answered. "But you, Master Becker, you're too strange. I'm more afraid of you. You may be one of *them*."

Chapter Nine

T*hem* . . . *them* . . . *them* . . . The word drummed in Jason's head. "Who do you mean by 'them'?"

Catherine Juliana shrugged off his question.

"Who are they?" He was almost yelling.

When the girl finally replied, Jason detected hate in her voice. "The Duke of Alba and his Council of Blood."

Alba? Three years of history in a private school, and never once did Jason have a whiff of the name *Alba*. Did he remember Alba from his Bruegel readings? Not really.

"You do know who he is, don't you?" she asked.

"No."

The silence between them hung heavy while she weighed Jason's answer. Then she scoffed. "Am I supposed to believe you aren't in league with Alba just because you tell me you don't know who he is? I'm not stupid! You could be lying just to get me to trust you."

"I don't care what you believe," Jason snapped. "I just want to get out of this tree, away from these killer dogs, and home again." Whoever they were, Alba and his Council of Blood weren't Jason's problem. Sixteenth-century bogeymen meant nothing to him. He belonged to the twenty-first century, and he was going to get back there.

Catherine squirmed, adjusting her back against the tree trunk as she watched him, and Jason wondered if maybe she halfway believed him.

"The Duke of Alba is a henchman for King Philip of Spain," she said.

"But this is Flanders, right? A long way from Spain."

"You act too dumb to work for Alba," she replied and made a "tsk, tsk" sound with her tongue. "Don't you really know that Spain rules Flanders and all the Netherlands?"

The sight of armed soldiers at the fair clicked into Jason's memory, and he grunted, a response she could take to mean yes or no.

Now the girl wouldn't let go of the topic, and Jason sensed both fear and hatred fomenting within her. "Alba's evil," she said. "His heart is black. He tortures his prisoners. And he kills them in horrible ways. He'll find me. I know he will."

Stop it! You're paranoid, he thought. *No king's henchman would bother with a little squirt like you. It's the blasted mastiffs that are the threat, not Alba.* But Jason kept such criticisms from reaching his lips, and when he did speak, he tried reassurance. "You're not his enemy. Alba doesn't care about you. You only stole some piddling guilders or whatever you call them. He wouldn't waste his time on you."

"You don't understand. He is after me."

Jason braced himself. What if it were true? Had Catherine Juliana done something else? His imagination conjured up all sorts of crimes the girl might have committed. He could easily see her shouting nasty words about the pope, sneaking messages to political prisoners, throwing rocks at the ducal residence. She was a nut, and Jason wouldn't put anything past her. "That *is* all you did, isn't it?" he demanded. "Steal a few guilders?" But he never got an answer. Catherine Juliana was asleep. Or pretended to sleep. He couldn't tell which.

When her head bobbed downward to rest on her chest, Jason took off his belt and long-sleeved shirt and, with one hand, clumsily tied them together into a makeshift rope. Careful not to wake her, he slipped the rope around her waist, securing her to the tree trunk so she wouldn't fall into the mouths below. His T-shirt wasn't enough to ward off the night's cold, but he didn't mind. Asleep, Catherine looked peaceful, almost pretty. It surprised him that he felt so protective of this loony kid. And for the first time, he was actually glad that he had saved her from the gallows.

His arms began to ache, and he loosened his hold on the tree so his blood could circulate more freely. There was nothing to do but wait.

The night stretched on. Now and then, a mastiff wandered off, but it always returned to join the others in a fierce canine ritual. The dogs circled and snarled and scratched at the tree's bark. Jason tried to master his fear by reliving past moments with Karen but couldn't, even though he had a storehouse of memories. His terror of the mastiffs shut out all else.

The not knowing if the mastiffs would go away, the not knowing if he would die at their mercy, that's what unnerved him. And as the hours crawled by, Jason discovered that waiting took a special brand of courage. In his mind, he died a dozen times in a dozen different ways. But he didn't die. He waited.

How can she sleep? he thought. Then he understood: Catherine Juliana had waited for her death before—on the gallows. Now she refused to wait again. So she had willed herself to sleep.

But he mustn't sleep. He mustn't fall.

He was grateful for the night's chill, which helped to keep him awake. His watch showed only 3:10 A.M. Weird, that it would be the same time here as it was back home. He'd save that puzzle for later. Now he pushed his watch into his jeans' pocket. It wouldn't be wise for the girl see it on his wrist; she was too suspicious already. Then he marveled that he thought his watch mattered, that he thought they'd live long enough for her to notice it.

In the moon's glow, he looked down at the massive dogs. Two had huge scars where the hair hadn't grown back; they'd probably been clawed by bears or gored by bulls and boars. The mastiffs didn't fight among themselves, and it struck Jason that they worked as a unit, pacing, growling, watching. And he knew they'd attack together, too.

Chapter Ten

Chilled and weary, Jason welcomed the breaking day from his perch in the tree. Dawn spread across the sky like a rose-colored fan feathered with clouds. Bird songs rode on the wind.

Below, three dogs growled. Where was the fourth? Jason hadn't seen it leave, but knew it would be back.

He looked at his waking "bride." Her hair hung in snarls, fatigue circled her eyes in raccoon rings, and every inch of her was filthy. At least she no longer wore that silly wedding wreath. He wondered what Karen looked like in the early morning. Gorgeous, he was sure.

"I'm grateful to you," said the girl when she saw herself tied to the tree's trunk. She loosened the makeshift rope and handed Jason his shirt and belt. "Did you sleep?"

"Enough," he answered.

"You're lying. You didn't sleep at all. I can tell."

Jason didn't deny it.

Then together, yet separately, they shared the waiting as the mastiffs prowled, angry and alert.

Less than an hour had gone by when Catherine Juliana touched Jason's arm and pointed downward.

The fourth dog had returned and now stood with head angled upward, smelling the air. The others mimicked its stance. Suddenly, all bolted into the trees, leaving only trampled greenery behind them.

"Other prey," said Catherine Juliana, who peered through the branches until the last tail had vanished from view. "Someone followed us. I told you that. The dogs have caught his scent. Maybe he's in a tree. Maybe not."

"How do you know it's another person?" Jason asked.

"I know," she answered. "And you would, too, if you lived anywhere around here, Master Becker."

"Maybe it's the pig from the fair."

She shook her head. "I don't think so."

When Jason started to climb down, Catherine Juliana gently put her hand on his shoulder and shook her head. "They might return. Let's wait to make sure."

"But we'll have a head start. We'll outrun them."

"Oh, Jason Becker, you are so stupid. How ever have you lived this long? The dogs would run us down."

The word *stupid* cut into Jason. His ego bristled. He couldn't remember anyone ever calling him stupid. Most people thought he was pretty smart. He had aced his SATs and his ACTs, and he had never missed the Parkman honor roll. Little good all that did him now.

He steeled his nerves to wait some more. At least the dogs were out of sight, not snarling below. And he relished the idea that he'd soon be rid of Catherine Juliana. Once safely on the ground, he'd see to that. But first he'd accompany her to where she lived. That only seemed proper.

With her out of the way, he'd be free to head for home. But how? The only plausible place for exiting this creepy century seemed to be the playground. After all, that's where he had arrived. In the mud. By rights, that's where he should leave from. But he had tried that. And it hadn't worked.

Then the answer slapped him. He *hadn't* tried to get

home from the *playground*. He'd tried to get home from the oak. He remembered scooting to the tree to get away from the kids. And the oak towered in the nearby field, not on the playground, and it wasn't in Bruegel's painting. No wonder He'd failed. Next time, he'd stand smack in the middle of the playground mud. That should get him home. Maybe. But maybe not. On the heel of his hopes came his doubts, too many of them. Even so, it was a good feeling to have a plan: He'd go back to the playground. His spirits rose.

The sun was high in the sky and the dogs had not returned, so the girl made her way to the ground, instructing Jason to follow. He did, but he skinned his nose on the tree trunk.

Catherine Juliana rolled her eyes. Jason did his best to walk quietly, stepping on the balls of his feet. He could have sworn that he heard her giggling.

She led, he followed, and they made their way back to the fields that bordered the woods. There they stopped.

"You go that way," she said, motioning toward the town, the fairground, the playground.

Jason shook his head. "No, I'll see you home first. Then I'll go." He wasn't in the habit of letting Karen go home alone, so now he felt obliged to accompany Catherine Juliana.

"Your choice," she said, shrugging her shoulders.

"Is it far?" he asked.

"Not far. And you can get some sleep at my place, then start home tomorrow. Your chances of getting through fields and woods are better in broad daylight—fewer predators on the prowl." At that, she smiled. Jason was surprised that her teeth were white and almost straight. "Where is your home, Jason Becker?" she asked.

"Stop calling me Jason Becker or Master Becker. Jason will do."

"And I am called Catherine."

"No, I'll call you Cat," he said. Catherine definitely didn't suit her, too elegant. She still reminded him of an alley cat, all gray and scrawny, but he couldn't tell her that, so he said, "Where I come from, Cat is short for Catherine."

"Fine," she said, stooping to break off the tops of new ferns that grew in damp soil beneath a tree. "I like the first fiddleheads. They're so tender." She stuffed one into her mouth and offered him one, too.

Jason shook his head. He wanted romaine with Caesar dressing. Even iceberg with his mom's no-fat French would do. But fiddleheads? He'd never heard of them.

Cat seemed to know all about the forest's edibles and about wild mastiffs and the Duke of Alba and everything else in this place. Jason knew next to nothing and that perturbed him. With a measure of self-importance, he asked, "Do you know Pieter Bruegel?"

"No." She continued to eat the fiddleheads.

Jason gloated, letting his chest swell a fraction.

"Who's Pieter Bruegel?" she asked.

"He's an artist from these parts."

"Maybe Papa knew him."

Yeah, your papa probably took his begging bowl to Bruegel's doorstep, he thought. But he said, "Someday Pieter Bruegel will be famous. Really famous. People will pay lots of money for his paintings."

"How would you know that?"

"I just know," Jason said smugly. But already he was ashamed of himself for wanting to show off.

"How do you know he'll be famous?" she repeated, narrowing her eyes. "And how do you know about Pieter Bruegel if you're not from around here?"

Jason felt trapped. "I made it all up," he mumbled, grabbing a fiddlehead and chomping off the top.

"Hmmm, hungry?" Cat said with a laugh. Then she ventured into the field to root about in the soil, ripping up new seedlings in the process. Jason didn't join her. She hadn't asked him to.

One by one, Cat dug up her finds and dropped them into Jason's jacket, which she had fashioned into a sack. "Wait 'til you see what I've got! Someone missed them at last year's harvest." She ran to Jason, displaying her treasures: seven withered turnips and four onions.

Jason hated turnips.

Cat again took the lead as they headed back into the trees. Swinging the sack, she rushed along a path barely visible beneath a web of vines and weeds. Farther and farther they went from the open fields, deeper and deeper into the woods. Jason's misgivings multiplied. If he couldn't find the fields again, he'd never find the playground. And without the playground, he'd never find the mud. And without the mud, he'd never know if that was his way home.

His thoughts were racing wildly—to Karen and how to get back to the twenty-first century—when he saw Cat sprint ahead and disappear through a break in the undergrowth.

"Hey, wait!" he yelled.

She didn't.

Chapter Eleven

Jason heard a loud splash as he tore after Cat. When he broke through the undergrowth, he was startled, pleasantly so. He stood in a small clearing with a pond in the center. Around it, wildflowers bloomed, yellow, purple, and white.

"Jump in," Cat called. "Drown your fleas."

She was neck-deep in water that shone clear as newly washed windows, her hair floating on its glassy surface. She still wore her shift but had placed her soft leather shoes neatly on the bank along with his jacket and the vegetables.

Jason watched her tear grass from the pond's edge and use it as a washcloth to clean her skin. Then she stepped out of the pond just long enough to pick twigs from a willow tree, new ones, soft and pliable. These served as her toothbrush. Last of all, she worked on her hair, scrubbing and dunking, scrubbing and dunking.

Jason was dumbfounded. The scrawny alley cat had transformed into a girl, a rather enchanting one, at that. Her hair was no longer gray from dust and dirt but the color of deep rust like autumn leaves, and her skin was very pale. Her high cheekbones now seemed even more prominent in her slender face. She wasn't gorgeous like Karen, but she had a strange sort of beauty, especially with those huge gray eyes.

"You best come in," she said. "Try to get rid of the fleas. And if you wash off the rest of the flour, you'll look less like a bun and more like a man."

Jason flushed with embarrassment. Thank goodness Karen couldn't see him. He knew he looked a sight, and stale ale made a lousy cologne. As for fleas, he was covered with bites.

He stripped to his waist, hiding his watch, pens, and notepads beneath his shirt, then plunged into the water. It was icy, but he didn't complain. If Cat could stand it, so could he. He tried to act as though this were something he did all the time, and he scrubbed with grass as Cat had done. But he thought maybe she wasn't fooled because she handed him some rougher grass, saying, "Here, this scrubs better."

When he felt reasonably clean, he returned to the bank and stretched out in the springtime sun. His jeans clung to his skin, clammy and cold. They'd take forever to dry, so he pressed his palms against the fabric, attempting to squeeze out the excess water. That didn't work, yet he didn't feel right about stripping to his shorts. He decided to stay miserable instead.

All the while, Cat played in the pond like a little kid. She inched . . . slowly . . . slowly . . . through the water toward a frog on a lily pad. She grabbed. She caught it! Then she kissed it and let it go.

As she climbed up the bank to where Jason basked in the sun, her shift snagged on a bush. The cloth tore, revealing a bony shoulder with a large red birthmark shaped like a skull.

"No," she cried. "I'm not. Truly I'm not." Frantically, she covered the mark with her hand.

"Not what?"

"I'm not a witch. I'm not," she whispered, almost pleading. Jason saw tears come to her eyes.

"I didn't say you were," he barked. Jason knew he'd never understand this girl.

"But you saw it. The witch mark."

"Don't be absurd," he said. "It's just a birthmark." He pulled her hand away. "Is that what you think this mark means, that you're a witch?"

"That's what people around here would think—if they saw it. Papa warned me never to let anyone see it."

"Well, to me, it's just a birthmark, nothing more," he said. "Besides, I don't believe in witches."

"It's easy to be branded a witch these days," she said. "Seems like people can accuse anyone, even poor old women who are bent and crippled or silly young girls who babble too much. You can't be too careful."

Jason went on sunning himself.

"When they accused me, I was afraid they'd see the mark," she said.

Jason looked at her, not understanding.

"At the hatmaker's, I didn't steal the guilders. They didn't belong to the hatmaker. They were mine," she said defensively. "But he screamed they were his, and he summoned the bailiff."

Cat's words poured out in a torrent. "I knew the bailiff wouldn't believe me. He said I stole, and he took me to the town tower. There were other men there, watching. They were going to strip me, take all my clothes. I was afraid they'd see the mark. The witch mark. So, I confessed before they could take my clothes. I said I stole the guilders, and they left me with this," she said, clutching at her shift. "It covered the mark. Nobody saw it. I fooled them." There was a note of triumph in her voice.

Jason couldn't believe what he was hearing. Catherine Juliana had confessed herself right into a hanging. She had signed her death warrant just to hide a silly birthmark. It didn't make sense. None of it did.

"I couldn't let them take *all* my clothes. You can understand that, can't you? The bailiff would have seen it." Cat touched the skull-shaped birthmark on her shoulder. "He would surely have called me a witch."

She sat down beside Jason, stretching out her legs. "Witches are always tortured so they'll name other witches. I don't know any witches. But I would have screamed names, anybody's name, just to make them stop torturing me. Then they would have burned me at the stake." Her voice was a whisper now. "Hanging seemed so much better, so much quicker. I should have gone to the gallows right away, but the bailiff wanted to keep me for May Day." She gave a low laugh, not of joy but of mockery. "The bailiff had no idea that Alba wanted me."

"How long did they keep you?" Jason asked.

She held up five fingers. "Five weeks in the town tower." Then she ran those fingers through her hair, fluffing out the long strands so that water droplets sprayed onto Jason.

"Hey," he said, and she laughed. Then the light moment vanished.

"The tower was damp and cold and there were lots of rats," she went on. "I could see the torturers. And I could see people suffering and dying. I don't even know why they were taken to the tower. Maybe some were supposed to be witches. But some weren't." Cat waited. "They all screamed, every one of them."

Her hands fluttered in the air as if she were trying to wave away scenes of the past. "The torturers tied down their victims. Then they used a big wooden wheel to batter their arms and legs until the flesh was bloody and the bones were smashed. And they—" She stopped. "I'm so sorry. I don't mean to give you ugly visions to carry around in your head. I shall never get rid of those pictures. I don't want you to have such memories, too."

Jason was grateful; he had heard enough. And he had already seen enough horrors in Flanders to last him a life-time.

Cat stood up, smoothed back her hair, and began to braid it into one long plait. When she finished, she looked down at Jason. "Alba tortures people, too. And he'll torture me if he gets me." For a brief moment, she smiled as though she had a joke all her own. "Alba's men never thought to look for me in the tower. All those weeks, I was right under their noses, and they didn't find me."

Inwardly, Jason cringed. More and more he believed that Alba was a phantom of Cat's imagination, that imprisonment had done something to her mind. It bothered him, too, that her tales of witches and torture would crouch forever in a dim corner of his brain.

Chapter Twelve

Jason bumbled behind Cat, who skillfully picked her way along a brambled path that snaked far into the woods. She was humming, and her high spirits annoyed Jason. He was grumpy.

You're happy because I don't think you're a witch, he thought. *You're happy because you know where you're going. Well, I'm not happy. I'm lost. I want to go home.*

"I can't see the path," he complained.

"You're just not used to it." Cat looked back and smiled at him. "It's an old deer track, overgrown now because there aren't many deer left," she explained. "I think they've been hunted out by man and beast."

Beast? Like what? Cat had told him there were boars. Wolves and bears, too? Jason decided not to ask because he really didn't want to know. The mastiffs were enough to worry about.

Spikes of sunlight poked through the treetops to light the way, but barely. The dimness made Jason skittish. The farther they walked, the closer the trees pressed around them, and the more the path narrowed until finally it was no wider than a city curb.

"Come on, Cat, stop."

She kept walking.

"Cat," he yelled. "I've got to get my bearings." He halted to look around. Each tree looked the same as the last and the next. They were all big with brown trunks, and they hemmed him in. How would he ever find this path again? "Stop. I'll never find my way back."

"You will," she said and kept walking.

"I won't."

"You will."

He wasn't reassured.

"I'll lead you out to the fields," she vowed, walking even faster.

Well, maybe you will, and maybe you won't. And maybe you'll just take off on your broomstick, and I'll never see you again. That'd be a break.

Jason decided not to rely on her follow-the-leader promise and pulled out his notepad while Cat's attention was elsewhere. He tore off several pages—quietly, so she wouldn't hear—and ripped the sheets into bits to mark the path. Then he backtracked, not far, and sprinkled paper here and there. He felt like Hansel lost in the woods, but Cat was no frightened Gretel. She was very sure of herself now.

Jason would have given anything for a street sign. A building. Graffiti. A stoplight. A movie marquee. Any of those wonderful landmarks from his century. He wished for a compass, too, although he admitted to himself that he didn't really know how to use one.

Strewing his bits of paper, he jogged to catch up with Cat. She was still humming and cradling the vegetable-filled jacket. At least she had mentioned nothing more about someone following them.

Then she said, "We've lost whoever was following us. Maybe to the mastiffs."

Jason clenched his jaw; his gratitude had come too soon. *What a loony,* he thought.

For a time, the two traveled without a word. But there was no silence. Jason heard rustlings and scratchings, and then a low snort that brought sweat to his forehead. He was used to car horns and sirens and cop whistles. Those sounds didn't spook him. The forest sounds did. He picked up his pace, moving closer to Cat and farther from the snort.

At intervals, he dropped his markers. And with every step, he agonized over the mess he was in. There had been times when he actually believed that he'd find his way back to his own century. But now he feared he might never escape Flanders. He tried to keep his doubts in check without success. Then he willed himself to walk without thinking, making his mind blank as an unchalked blackboard.

He stared at Cat's braid swaying to and fro, as mesmeric as a pendulum. Gradually, drowsiness washed over him.

The girl turned to see him yawn. "You can sleep when we get there. I slept last night; you didn't. And we'll eat. We can mix the onions and turnips."

"I don't like turnips. . . . I can't eat them. . . . They upset my stomach," Jason announced, his words strung out like barbed wire.

"Then you can share Charles's dinner," she said.

Charles? Who was Charles? Her beggar father? But she always seemed to speak of him in the past tense. A brother? Friend? Husband? *I'm her husband.* That thought gagged him. *No! I'm not her husband. Maybe Charles is a lover? Hardly! She's too young. Too skinny.*

Well, if he was forced to share quarters with another male, Jason wanted to know who it was. "Who's Charles?" he demanded. The question came out just short of a shout.

"You'll meet him," she answered.

More and more, Jason was feeling less and less in control of his fate. And now this Charles was in the offing. He thought of the men at the fairground and shuddered. He didn't relish another confrontation with the likes of them.

But he could handle it, he assured himself. After all, he *did* get Cat off the gallows. Besides, there would be only one peasant this time. Not dozens. Jason's black mood mellowed to gray. With his eyes half closed, he stumbled along behind the bobbing braid, a trail of markers behind him.

Suddenly, he bumped into Cat, who had stopped to pluck a long, broad blade of grass. She smoothed it, then sandwiched it between her two thumbs, holding her fingers in a loose prayer position. Her eyes sparkled, not with joy but mischief—definitely mischief. She brought the grass blade to her mouth and blew. The resulting whistle echoed off the treetops like the sound of a far-off foghorn.

Jason detected a grin behind her hands. She blew again. Then again. After a minute's wait, she repeated the three blasts.

"Just a signal," she said.

"Who for?" Jason was sure she was giggling.

"For Charles, of course. I want him to know I'm home. He's probably been frightfully worried about me."

"Oh, I'm sure," said Jason. If her Charles was so worried, why hadn't *he* tried to rescue her? Some hero. Jason let the subject drop and plodded along, falling farther and farther behind Cat, not because he was tired but because he was peeved. He knew if he stayed close on her heels, he'd shout something nasty about her and Charles. Why had he offered to see Cat home, anyway? She didn't need him. She had Charles.

He stopped to tie his shoe and to check behind him to make sure his markers were well spaced. He counted five in plain view.

When he turned around again, he froze. In the distance, he saw a mastiff tearing toward Cat. "Climb!" he yelled. But he didn't climb himself. Instead, he picked up the biggest stick in sight and rushed toward her.

He shouted at her again, but it was too late. The dog was

upon her, its paws on her shoulders. They both went down, a tangle of fur and legs.

Jason was close now, his stick raised. But he never delivered the blow.

The dog was licking. And Cat was laughing.

"Meet Charles," she said, peering over the dog's head. Then she scrambled to her feet.

Jason didn't know whether to be quietly indignant or loudly furious. In the end, he did neither. He was so relieved that he could only laugh.

Charles growled.

"Friend, Charles, friend," Cat ordered. Instantly, the dog, with wagging tail, trotted to Jason, snuffling and drooling. He nuzzled Jason's hand.

"He likes you," said Cat happily. "He really does."

"Please tell me he didn't belong to that killer pack," Jason said, wiping the slobber from his hands and jeans.

"Heavens no," said Cat. "Poor thing, he was almost dead when I found him. He'd been gored. See?" She traced her fingers along a scar on the dog's side. "A boar got him. I'm sure he was a guard dog, but he must have gone out with a hunting party. How cruel to have left him behind to die." She threw her arms around the dog's neck and buried her face in his fur. "You're so skinny, Charles," she admonished. "Haven't you been hunting your supper? Jason Becker here wants to share with you. He doesn't like turnips."

"I *love* turnips," said Jason. "Love them." He could just see Charles bringing him mangled rabbits and squirrels, mice and grasshoppers, all slobbery. He'd eat turnips if they killed him.

In a million years, Jason could not see himself being friends with this beast. He wasn't used to dogs. After all, he had been raised in a high-rise, hardly a dog's domain. The dogs he had encountered were leashed and groomed, and they pranced along city streets with ribbons on their ears.

Not Charles. Like the other mastiffs, he had a big head, a massive body, and eyes that were sharp and fierce. Besides all that, he drooled constantly. Jason tested the dog's friendship with a quick pat—just one—on the furry head, then withdrew his hand.

"Let's go home," said Cat to Charles. The two romped down the path, the vegetables still swinging in the makeshift sack.

Home? Not home! Lodging for the night. Never home, Jason thought as he trailed behind the pair.

Chapter Thirteen

The sight of Cat's home didn't shock Jason in the least. By now he was ready for anything.

As he looked at the hovel, a merry-go-round of memories spun in his head, of motels and hotels where he had stayed, deluxe places with swimming pools and saunas and hot showers with new bars of soap every day. Such memories seemed like fantasies now.

Cat and Charles had already disappeared inside, but Jason dawdled outside, in no hurry to enter such a hovel. To him, Cat's home was a mud hut, crude at best, carelessly thrown together and topped with a roof of thatch. Then he reconsidered. A chunk of mud had fallen away from the hut's exterior, and he saw an underlying construction of twigs and branches meticulously interlaced. He acknowledged it did take a certain amount of know-how to build such a frame.

A small clearing spread out in a semicircle in front of the hovel. The land was dotted with rotting tree stumps, still showing old scars from an axe. The area was free of heavy undergrowth, too. Jason wondered who kept all that vegetation from growing back. Did Cat do that?

He tilted his head to study the hovel's wooden door. It was lopsided. And no wonder. Instead of hanging on hinges, it swiveled on a single thick peg at its top, another at its bottom, and the pegs were sadly out of line. But the door did open and close—although with a creak and a groan.

Jason went inside.

The hut was dim even though Cat had shoved open the wooden shutters to let sunlight squeeze through two tiny windows. There were no glass windowpanes, so bugs and bats were free to come and go. The floor was dirt that had been packed to the hardness of cement. And the whole place was no bigger than Jason's bedroom at home.

"Don't nap yet," Cat said, handing him a broom. "You sweep out and make tidy. I've got to get the planting done." She took seeds from earthenware jars sitting in rows on a wooden shelf, each jar scratched with a symbol. "The beans and cabbage. Lettuce and beets. They should have been sown by now." She kept the seeds separate, putting some in her shoes and holding some in her hands.

Jason opened the door for her and watched the sunlight play on her face. He was troubled by what he saw. Her cheeks were flushed, her eyes too bright, and spangles of sweat glistened on her forehead.

He started to voice his concern. "Cat, don't you think you should rest and—"

She didn't let him finish. "We'll eat when the sun sets. There's a stream over there, right beyond the clearing." She jerked her head in the direction. "You can wash the turnips there."

From that, Jason assumed he was to fix a meal, too. He was slightly nonplussed by his list of chores. At home, his mom had a maid and a cook to do these things.

He watched Cat run the short stretch to a vegetable patch. There, she placed the seeds in neat piles on the ground. Then she returned to grab a hoe and spade that leaned against the hovel. Charles never left her side. Running again, she called a warning over her shoulder, "Keep watch. Someone still might be following us."

Jason scowled.

He gave the broom a hard swish as he stepped back inside to take stock of the place. Against one wall, a long wooden box held a mattress, partially covered with sheepskins. The mattress looked lumpy, and Jason peeked inside the open end to find it stuffed with dried autumn leaves. A large chest took up much of another wall. He was tempted to lift its lid but didn't.

He walked around a trestle table to the wooden loom that stood in a corner. Next to it was a three-legged stool topped with a red woolen blanket, neatly folded. Jason fingered the blanket, finding it extremely soft, too lovely for the impoverished setting. He wondered if Cat had made it.

Dutifully, if not expertly, he swept around the furniture, ducking his head to avoid herbs that hung in bunches from a crossbeam. He couldn't name a single herb but was pleased with their mixed scent, which made the hovel smell cleaner than it was.

There was no fireplace, merely a fire circle in the middle of the room with an iron kettle hanging from a crook. By the door, firewood was stacked next to a big basket filled with lumps of brown stuff that Jason guessed was peat.

He heaved a sigh. Plenty of campers in his century had it better than this.

Along a wall, a meager array of clothes dangled from wooden pegs. But they weren't all girls clothes. There were two long brown tunics and a hooded cloak that belonged unmistakably to an adult male. On the floor sat large wooden clogs, big enough for a horse of a man.

Someone else did live here! That's who probably pulled up all the undergrowth outside, not Cat. Jason didn't know why he was furious, but he was, and he grabbed one of the tunics and stomped out the door.

He found Cat hoeing in the garden. "Who else lives here?" he demanded.

"No one."

He held up the tunic that was twice Cat's size. "And I suppose you wear this?"

"It's the hermit's."

"And just where is *he* sleeping tonight?" Jason's tone was colder than a winter blast.

Cat put down her hoe and pointed to a small wooden cross on a mound of rocks, almost hidden by bushes at the clearing's edge. "There. Where I buried him."

Jason stared at her as another piece of her life's puzzle fell into place. "This isn't really your home, is it?" He should have known that Cat's cultivated speech and demeanor hadn't been molded within a mud hovel.

"No, I found it. I was hiding from Alba. There was no place to go. I couldn't seek out those I knew because Alba would seize them, too. For days I hid in the trees and ate roots. Then, one morning, there it was, the hermit's home, deep in the woods, far from *them*. I thought it was a miracle." Her voice was low and mellow as gold. "I thought God had given me a place to stay."

She smiled at Jason, an apologetic sort of smile. "I didn't think the hermit would care if I moved in. He was quite dead when I arrived. He smelled dreadful."

Jason imagined her dragging the body out of the hut and across the clearing. He wondered if he could have done the same.

He smoothed her hair off her forehead, then lifted her face so he could see into her eyes. But she looked down. "Cat, please tell me what you did. Why do you have to hide here? Is there really an Alba, or are you just making him up? Tell me, Cat. You owe it to me. I did save your life."

"Yes, I do owe you an explanation. But what about you, Jason? You drew my picture with a strange instrument on paper that's finer and smoother than any I've ever seen. You hide those things. And what about the bracelet that you wore on your wrist? You hide that, too. And the style of your clothes and the buttons on your jacket. Where are you from, Jason?"

He didn't answer.

Cat let her shoulders slump. She was shivering. "Go. I must finish." Her voice no longer commanded but begged. "Starvation is real here, Jason. Maybe not where you come from, but here, it is. I must plant now. I don't want to; I'm tired, and I'm cold, but I must. Later, we'll eat and we'll talk. I promise."

Jason didn't argue and walked slowly back to the hovel.

Once inside again, he decided Cat needed something hot. Turnip stew? He liked that idea. He pulled dry leaves— not many—from the mattress. These he'd use as kindling, and he stuffed them beneath the wood and peat that he'd stacked tepee-style within the fire circle. Then his palm slapped his forehead in disgust. No matches! In this time and place, matches were a marvel of the future. But there had to be something to get a fire going.

Jason found what he needed on the shelf, stashed behind the seed pots: a flint, an iron ring, and a small metal box. A good half hour came and went before he figured out how to use his fire-making tools. He knew a Boy Scout would have nailed the technique in a minute, and that made him angry. Clumsily, he struck the flint against the iron ring until sparks flew. The trick, he soon learned, was to get the sparks to drop onto bits of charred cotton stored within the metal tinder box. He got sparks, all right. But they sprayed everywhere except where they were supposed to. He tried. And tried. Eventually, a few sparks hit the cotton. Jason puckered his lips and blew gently. The cotton began to glow red. From the broom, he plucked a straw and held it next to the smoldering cloth until it flickered like a match.

Jason had fire.

He stuck the straw into the autumn leaves. They flared up, igniting his pyramid of wood and peat. For good measure, he took off his socks and tossed them in, too. He figured they'd burn quickly.

The fire soon blazed. And Jason was proud, certain that Daniel Boone could have done no better. He watched the smoke spiral neatly upward, disappearing through a black-edged hole in the roof.

While his turnip-and-onion stew simmered, he picked a dozen daisies that bloomed at the wood's edge. He stuck them in an empty seed pot to serve as a centerpiece. Next, he tossed a fern salad with a liberal share of herbs. Then, to his delight, he discovered a chunk of honeycomb in an earthenware crock. Dessert!

By the time the sun slid beneath the horizon, Jason had set the table with two wooden bowls, two wooden spoons, and the only knife he could find. He decided to give the lone stool to Cat.

The fire crackled, and the hut took on a cozy warmth, shutting out the cool evening air. Jason added more peat to make the blaze brighter. He listened to the flames hiss and snap while shadows cavorted on the walls.

For the first time since arriving in Flanders, he basked in a sense of well-being. He heard two light thumps as Cat put the hoe and spade against the hut. The door opened.

Jason smiled.

But Cat didn't look at him. Nor at the supper table. Nor at the daisies. She stared only at the fire. Then she slumped into a heap on the cold dirt floor.

Chapter Fourteen

Long into the night, Jason sat beside Cat's bed. She was burning up, tossing from side to side on her lumpy leaf mattress, wildly delirious. He didn't know what to do, how to help her. Then, sometime after midnight, he realized there was nothing he could do but wait and watch and bathe her forehead in cool water.

He studied her face, her neck and arms. The skin was smooth and white. There were no swellings, no black splotches, and a wave of gratitude swept over him. In his European history class he had read about the plague and its hideous effects. If only the Black Death had died in the fourteenth century along with its thousands and thousands of victims. But it hadn't. Jason wished such historical facts weren't stored in his brain, but there they were, gnawing at him like rodents' teeth. He pulled up his pant legs to look at the flea bites, knowing full well the plague was spread by fleas and rats.

With a strange kind of relief, Jason realized that he had been so afraid so many times in the past day and night that he was now conditioned. Fear no longer chained him. It attacked him, yes, making his knees weak and his mouth dry, but he now knew how to stay calm, forging onward despite fear's onslaughts.

He considered praying but to his dismay discovered he didn't know a single prayer and couldn't remember any Bible verses. He did believe in God, but in his life of comfort and privilege, that belief had not been tested. Back home, he sometimes went to church with friends but never with his mom and dad or Karen. Now, as he held Cat's hand, he made up his own prayer, talking quietly to the invisible Infinite, trusting that Cat would get well.

In her delirium, Cat called to her father, "I promise, Papa. I promise. I will, Papa. I promise," until Jason thought he could not bear to hear her cry out again. Through the hours, he said her name time and time again, but she never answered.

The shutters kept the night's blackness from invading the cottage, while inside, the fire's embers burned blood red. Jason found the stubs of two tallow candles on the shelf but decided to save them. He had no need for brighter light because there was nothing he could do other than wait.

Through the trying hours, Charles never left Cat's side, sometimes sleeping on the dirt floor, sometimes sitting and resting his head on the mattress. Big as he was, he moved lightly without whine or bark.

When dawn came, there was no change in Cat's condition. She looked pathetically thin, with deep shadows beneath her eyes. Her hair was damp with sweat. Jason tried to get her to drink water that he had carried from the stream. She wouldn't. She responded to nothing.

By midmorning, despite his growing concern, Jason was ravenous with hunger. Last night's meal had gone uneaten, and he now shared it with Charles, even the honeycomb. The turnip-and-onion stew was not good but not bad either. Jason was so hungry and so worried about Cat, that taste and texture didn't matter. Afterward, he took up his vigil again. Cat no longer tossed or cried out but now lay motionless.

As the morning dragged into afternoon, Jason found himself alternating between his own brand of prayer and a monologue of reminiscences. He knew Cat couldn't hear him, so he felt free to talk about what he knew, what he felt. He rambled about Karen and Chicago, about airplanes and cars, about computers and skyscrapers and factories that could make millions of dresses in a month and machines that could harvest hundreds of acres in a single day. He talked about his school and his mom and dad and how he wanted to be an artist, not a lawyer. He told how his parents believed art was fine for a Sunday hobby but demanded law for a career, how he had satisfied them by applying to Harvard. He confided, too, that he had secretly sent an application to the Rhode Island School of Design. Not even Karen knew that.

Although Cat heard nothing of what he was saying, Jason felt obliged to mention the bad with the good. He spoke about the two world wars and how the A-bomb had leveled whole cities. Mostly, though, he told her about pretty things: the paintings in the Art Institute, the symphonies that thundered in Orchestra Hall, the millions of books in public libraries, and the fountain in downtown Chicago that sprayed water in rainbow colors.

He talked until he could talk no more, then laid his head on the edge of the mattress and slept.

It was dark when he awoke. Cat remained motionless. But he heard her still breathing.

For the first time in hours, Jason left her side and opened the door to look upward at a sky filled with stars, flickering like a million fireflies. He couldn't remember ever taking time to stare up at the stars for the sheer wonder of it all. Besides, in the city, the blaze of neon blocked out much of the celestial scene.

By midnight, he was hungry again, but there was no food in the hovel. He and Charles had eaten everything, down to the last limp fern. What if Cat awoke and was hungry?

Jason lit a candle stub and carried it to her bedside. Her cheeks were hollow and her arms looked even thinner than before. He had to get food into her. Broth, that's what she needed. He'd spoon it down her the minute she awoke.

But for broth he needed chicken. Bread would be good, too, and fruit and an egg or two. He made his decision quickly: He'd go shopping in the town. He'd probably have to visit separate vendors, but that shouldn't take too long. At first light, he'd follow his markers and run most of the way. Cat wouldn't even know he was gone, and Charles would watch over her.

In a burst of energy, Jason grabbed one of the hermit's tunics from a wooden peg and tried it on. A passable fit. Then he took down the cloak. He liked the hood that could be pulled over his head to hide his twenty-first-century haircut. The clogs were a bit big but surprisingly comfortable. With a little luck, he just might blend in among the townspeople.

The forty-three dollars in his jeans were obviously worth less than lettuce in sixteenth-century Flanders. And he was wise enough to know that he shouldn't deal with Flemish currency—even if he had a bundle of it. His ignorance of its worth would certainly attract attention. No, money wouldn't work. He needed to barter. But a glance around the room showed not a single thing worth lugging to town to trade. For a moment, he stared at the chest. Then he crossed his fingers and threw open the lid, shuffling through its contents: one shuttle for the loom, two needles, gray thread wound around a wooden rod, a small ball of red yarn, a tallow candle, and a crude pair of scissors. The entire lot probably wouldn't bring much more than a loaf of bread.

Dejected, Jason sat by the fire, searching the flames as though the answer lay within. His brain felt fogged, and no solution surfaced. It was more than an hour later when a plan finally formed. But he needed sixteenth-century art materials to carry it out: a quill pen, ink, and rough paper or parchment. His own pens and pad were quite useless in this time and place.

Slowly, he pulled the class ring from his finger. It was sapphire with a gold setting and the Parkman High motto, "Peace and Wisdom," inscribed in Latin in fancy script: "Pax et Sapientia." Would it arouse suspicion? Maybe. Maybe not. The risk was there, but he'd take it. He'd trade the ring for quill and parchment; then he'd sketch the butcher, the baker, the basket maker, whoever was willing to give him food in return. It might work. And on that frail hope, he fell asleep.

Chapter Fifteen

Jason took a last look at Cat, then closed the hovel door and hurried into the woods. In the early light, his markers stood out like bits of cotton amid the springtime green, and he trotted from one to the next, his confidence intact.

But fear soon wormed around inside him as the trees crowded closer. He knew the killer dogs could be lurking. He listened, well aware that he hadn't heard the mastiffs before, in the stillness of night. Was there even a chance that he'd hear them now? The sounds of morning—the scurrying of small creatures and the calling of birds—were certain to cover the dogs' footfalls. He quickened his pace, always keeping in sight a tree that he could climb.

His paper trail gave out near the pond where he and Cat had scrubbed themselves clean. From there on, he had to pick his way blindly along the overgrown path, muttering and swearing and watching for the mastiffs. When he finally broke out of the woods onto the open field, he did mental flips. He had found his way—and the dogs hadn't found him. A better victory than winning a gymnastics' gold, he decided.

New sprouts blanketed the fields, and he saw where Cat had unearthed last year's turnips, the ground still disturbed around her digging. The field was too open for comfort, so he walked along the woods' edge until the fairground came into view. It was empty now. Close by it ran the major lane that led to town. That's where he headed.

The thoroughfare already bustled with early risers who wore caps and jackets to ward off the morning chill. Most were on foot, some on donkeys, a few in carts. Jason joined the throng but not before he had pulled up the hood of his cloak to shield his head from curious eyes.

He shared the lane with all sorts of travelers, many burdened with the trappings of their trade. There were makers of shoes, menders of worn-out clothes, fixers of broken furniture, sellers of rags, and beggars of morsels. Along with them went the women who carried marketing baskets.

All streamed across the canal bridge, the waters below throwing off a stench of refuse and sewage. But Jason paid no mind. He was thinking back to three days ago when the children had herded him across this very bridge. Off to the right, he spotted the huge oak that towered near the playground. He couldn't see the mud pit, but he knew it was there, waiting for him. He could go there now and try to get home. It was tempting.

But what about Cat?

He had already saved her life once. Maybe that was enough. Besides, there was no guarantee that he could help her now, even if he did get food.

Then Jason pictured her lying on the mattress, no one to watch over her, or worse yet, waking hungry and alone, wondering if he would return.

He stepped off the bridge and walked straight into town.

By Jason's standards, it wasn't much of a town, a few dirt streets with offshoot alleys here and there. From his Bruegel reading, he knew at least one alley led to the butcher's and the tanner's. He'd stay away from there. Such trades were always relegated to the outskirts because the smells from tanning hides and slaughtering animals were too much for even the sixteenth-century nose.

He trudged through the street's muck in his low-slung clogs, past narrow houses rising to three stories, some made of stone, some of brick, many of wood. High above him, a plump-faced woman leaned from a window and emptied a chamber pot. Jason leaped aside. The slop rained past him, splashing onto the muddy street to rot amidst the garbage and donkey droppings. Pigs rooted in the refuse. Rats scuttled through it.

All along the street, wooden signs creaked in the breeze, each advertising the craft within a house. Jason glanced through open doors where craftsmen worked. Outside, shelves and stalls displayed their finished products: copper kettles, crockery, tinware, and tapestries. Jason didn't tarry at any of these because time was fleeting.

But then, he stopped short. An art gallery! Without even thinking, he went inside. His heart skipped. Surrounded by an array of nondescript paintings, he saw an oil of hunters and their dogs on a hilltop, laboring through snow. Jason recognized the masterpiece at once. A Bruegel—one of the most famous snow scenes ever painted.

He stood before it.

"Pieter Bruegel painted that one," said the proprietor, coming from behind a curtain. "I think it's rather good, don't you?" His speech was cultured, his attire impeccable.

"*Very* good," said Jason.

"We used to get more from Master Bruegel when he lived in Antwerp. But he's in Brussels now."

The proprietor looked down to refasten a hook on his fur-trimmed doublet. As he did, Jason reached toward the painting. His fingertips traced, ever so lightly, across the snowy terrain. No museum guards rushed toward him. No alarms went off.

The proprietor looked up. "Are you interested in the painting?" he asked, surveying Jason's shabby cloak.

"Only to love it—and leave it." Jason pivoted and walked out the door.

He couldn't believe he had done that—touched a Bruegel painting. *Pieter Bruegel is here, living and breathing. In this century. At this very moment. He's so close.* Then Jason's thoughts of the artist dissolved as he looked ahead. Right beyond the town tavern stood the hatmaker's house, a dozen hats jumbled together on an outside shelf. This was where Cat had been caught. Why had she been inside? He had no answers and moved on, past the blacksmith, the tailor, and the jewelry maker. A shiver passed through him when he saw a swinging sign that proclaimed the man within was both barber and surgeon. A lute hung outside the door so clients could wile away their waiting time with a tune. Jason heard no music today, only a howl of pain.

At a brisk pace, he explored all the streets and most of the alleys, but nowhere did he see a merchant who sold parchment or paper, quill and ink. He sneaked a look at his watch. Nine o'clock. He wanted to be back by noon.

He stood at a loss and gazed at the Catholic church. It had been built on a rise, easy for all to see. Jason had visions of monks hunched over manuscripts, painstakingly copying Bible passages with feathered quills. He knew that such copying took place in monasteries, not the local churches. Nevertheless, he'd give the church a try. What could he lose?

He followed two elderly women through the massive church doors. Each toted a small folding stool, and when Jason's eyes adjusted to the church's dim interior, he understood why: There were no benches or pews for the ordinary people.

By the altar, a priest was lighting tapers. Even from the

back of the church, Jason could tell this wasn't the frail old priest who had performed the gallows ceremony. No, this priest was younger, a pudgy man in a long brown robe. Jason strode boldly to the chancel, his clogs clacking on the stone floor. The priest turned to show a sour face without the smile and twinkling eyes that so often go with a rotund body. The priest's lips were thin and taut as wire.

Jason reached beneath his cloak and retrieved the ring. The priest's eyes widened at the sight of gold and sapphire. His chubby fingers reached out, but Jason held tight to his possession.

"The ring, good Father, is yours—if I may have writing materials in return."

"Ahh, you must be a copyist. Do you copy tradesmen's ledgers?" the priest asked. The odor of onions hung on his breath.

Jason shook his head.

The priest waited.

"I sketch," Jason said.

"And who will you sketch? I know everyone in town."

Jason shrugged.

"You're not from here, I can see." The priest examined Jason from hood to clogs.

"No, not from here," Jason said.

"Well, where from, my boy?"

"Far off," Jason snapped, and he could feel himself starting to sweat.

The priest smiled. The candles flickered, worshippers prayed, and Jason wished he were somewhere else.

"Interesting. An artist from far away who's going to sketch but doesn't know who or what."

"Will you trade?" Jason asked, his voice too loud.

"Of course, my boy, of course," said the priest, rubbing his fat fingers up and down Jason's arm.

The bargaining began. And for a good ten minutes, the

two haggled as though the church were a bazaar instead of a holy house. In the end, Jason turned his back to disengage his watch from its fourteen-karat band. Hiding the watch in his hand, he reluctantly threw the band into the bargain. The priest smiled an oily smile.

When Jason left the church, he carried parchment made from sheepskin, goose-quill pens, horns of ink, and a goat's tooth to polish the finished parchment. He now had what he needed to get food for Cat.

But he was haunted by the priest's actions: too many questions, too many "my boy" endearments, too many smiles that bordered on smirks. And the thought of the priest pawing his arm made him wince.

Chapter Sixteen

The woman stood outside the church, waiting for him. She was bone thin with wisps of white in her dark hair. When Jason saw her, he felt a flicker of recognition. But whom could he possibly know in the sixteenth century?

He wanted to run but couldn't; his feet were leaden, his mind flustered. Then a shred of memory surfaced. The waffle woman from the fair, that's who she was. He remembered her hair and her slender figure, and, most of all, her gentleness in that raucous scene, a dove amid magpies.

She approached him. "I am Griet," she said quietly, yet with the confidence of one accustomed to having authority. "I first saw you at the gallows, and today I saw you in church." She hesitated, smiling slightly. "I wish to thank you. I thank you for saving Catherine Juliana." Her words were well spoken, without the peasants' twang.

Jason didn't know what to say, so he waited.

"Quite a lady you wedded," she said.

"Hardly a lady. She's the daughter of a beggar." Immediately Jason regretted the comment. His words had been truthful—but unkind—and he realized for the first time that he never wanted to be unkind to Cat again.

"Don't be a fool," said Griet.

Jason took the reproof like a slap and knew he deserved it.

"What do you know of Catherine Eijngaard? What do you know of her father?" Griet was indignant.

Jason admitted he knew little.

"Yes, Master Eijngaard was a Beggar but not a beggar of the streets," said Griet. "Do you not know the difference?"

Jason shook his head.

"Listen closely," she said. "Master Eijngaard belonged to a special group of men who resist Spain's oppression. They call themselves the Beggars, and they adopted the beggar's wooden bowl as their symbol."

Jason tried his best to digest this news. But why hadn't Cat told him this? Why had she let him think that her father groveled in the street for his daily bread? Then it occurred to Jason that Cat didn't trust him enough to explain.

"Most of the Beggars are of noble birth," Griet said. "Not Master Eijngaard. But he was wealthy, one of the wealthiest merchants in Antwerp. Since he shared the nobles' cause, they welcomed him into their fold."

Passersby slowed to look at the two of them talking, and Jason grew uneasy. "Let's walk," he suggested.

As they ambled along, Griet spoke quietly. "The Beggars are against religious persecution and foreign rule in the Netherlands. Some have even denounced the Church and Pope, secretly following other religious teachings."

A sadness came to her eyes, and she glanced at the Catholic church behind her, shaking her head. "Master Eijngaard chose to follow Martin Luther's teachings. He supported the rights of the Baptists and the Calvinists, too. I fear he was none too private about his views," she lamented. "Alba arrested him, and Master Eijngaard was charged with heresy against the Catholic Church."

"That's why Catherine ran away?" Jason's words were half question, half statement.

"She was right to run," said Griet. "In the name of the king of Spain, the master's country estate was confiscated—hectares and hectares of land. His house in Antwerp, too."

"Is that where Catherine lived? On all that land? And in Antwerp?" Jason was careful not to call her Cat in front of Griet.

"Ahhh, the country house. What a place! That was their main home. It was on open land outside of Antwerp. Not far from this town, either." Griet looked down and daintily navigated around a large puddle of muck without missing a verbal beat. "I was hired to manage the Eijngaard household after the master's wife died. For fourteen years, I took care of the country house, and I watched Catherine grow into a lady.

"Sometimes we stayed in Antwerp," she said, "but that was mainly the master's place of business. Catherine always adored the excitement of the city."

"You love Catherine, don't you?" he said.

Griet's eyes grew misty. "How could I not love her? When she fled, I tried my best to find her. Then I saw her at the gallows."

Jason reached out to pat Griet's arm as she brushed away a single tear. Then quickly, she masked her face with indifference. "The master had thirty weavers living on his land. He held the cloth trade of Antwerp in his palms." Griet held out her open hands, flicking her fingers. "But he's gone, and our work is finished. Now I live with my brother and sell waffles and wear mended clothes."

Bits and pieces of Cat's actions suddenly made sense to Jason, although his thoughts about her were still a jumble.

"I give you warning," Griet said. "Alba's men are looking for Catherine. Get her away."

"Why do they want her? She's not a Beggar, she's just a girl."

"I don't know why they're hunting her. It's a mercy they didn't find her in the town tower."

"Catherine tried to tell me she was being hunted, and I didn't believe her." Jason's conscience ached.

Griet lowered her voice again, now whispering. "We're being watched by everyone who passes. Who knows what spy might be among them."

They continued slowly down the uncobbled street, allowing no emotion to show on their faces. "I have a sister in Paris," she said. "She would take you in, at least for a while. In France, Catherine would be safe from Alba."

"Paris? France?" The words hung on Jason's lips.

"Don't worry," Griet said. "I can lead you there, but we must leave at once."

Jason couldn't help himself. He hugged this woman who was trying so desperately to help her beloved Catherine.

Then he backed away. "She can't travel. She's ill with fever."

"Swellings? Black spots?"

"No," Jason answered, "it's not the plague. Just a roaring fever from fright and fatigue and too little to eat in the tower."

"Then you must put a spider's head in a clamshell and hang it about her neck," Griet advised.

Jason tried to keep the doubt from his eyes.

"Do it," she said. "It will take away the fever. Catherine knows that."

Although skeptical of such a sixteenth-century remedy, Jason agreed. He'd try anything that Cat believed. He'd buy a clam in the village, and he'd find a spider in the woods.

The two walked to the street's edge and stood by the tailor's shop. No one went in, and no one came out; nevertheless, Jason spoke in a hush. He explained about the flight to the hovel and how Cat had gone out to plant. "I thought she was all right. I really did. While she worked in the garden, I swept up and started supper, and I made a nice fire to brighten up the hut and take off the chill. I should never have let her plant. She must have been too weak. I should have done the hoeing and digging."

"No fault of yours," said Griet, but her words failed to lift the blame that Jason carried like a sack of stones. "Yes, she was weak, but the work didn't affect her. It was the flames."

Jason didn't understand. "She didn't even come near the fire."

"The very sight was more than she could bear," Griet said. "That's what made her ill."

Jason waited. There was more, he knew, remembering how Cat had never faced the bonfire at the fair.

"Fire is the final terror for Catherine," Griet explained. She took a deep breath. "Alba burned Master Eijngaard at the stake—while Catherine watched from the crowd."

Chapter Seventeen

Jason stumbled down the street, clutching his parchment and quills. He had agreed to see Griet again in just three days' time. They'd meet at her brother's house on the outskirts of town, and there, they'd plot an escape to Paris. Neither had voiced the fear that Cat might not be well enough to travel, but Jason had thought it, and he knew the same concern must have crossed Griet's mind, too.

All he could think about was Cat. Alba was after her. She hadn't invented that. Why hadn't he listened to her?

He looked at his watch, which he now had to carry in his hand. Almost eleven. He still didn't have a single morsel of food. What if Cat woke up and he wasn't there? She'd think he had deserted her, left her to die. The urge to hurry overwhelmed him.

With a fleeting wish for plastic shopping bags, he looked around. He needed something in which to tote his food, his art supplies, his watch. Just beyond the market area, he spied an old woman sitting on the ground amid heaps of baskets, some little, some big, all tightly woven from reeds and vines.

She looked ancient. Her hair was dirty white, her face webbed with wrinkles. Jason felt an ounce of pity. His mistake—she bargained better than a merchant half her age. When all was said and done, Jason considered himself lucky to get two baskets for three sketches. In his drawings, he erased years from the woman's face by leaving out a crease here, a line there. He curled her hair a bit, too. At the sight of herself on parchment, she snorted. Then she gave him a grin of gaps and teeth. And a wink.

Jason wanted no nosy people watching him shop and sketch, so he searched for vendors who weren't thronged with buyers. That wasn't always wise. There were tradesmen whose business was slow for a very good reason: Their products were shoddy or spoiled.

Right off, he noticed a fishmonger smearing pig's blood on the gills of cod to make the stale fish look fresh. He skipped that stall. Then he saw two women point fingers at a seller who had soaked his cheese in broth. The two complained, yapping to all within earshot that the broth made inferior cheese appear rich and creamy. They refused to buy. So did Jason.

He was delighted to discover that bartering was second nature to these people. Whenever coins were in short supply, they were more than ready to swap this for that—ducks for shoes, piglets for grain, loaves for nails. And to Jason's good fortune, vendors welcomed his sketches.

A horn blasted from a nearby house. Jason trailed a flock of women until the aroma of bread, hot and fresh from the oven, tickled his nose and told him he was at the baker's. When the last buyer had left with her basketful of baked goods, Jason stepped forward to bargain. Only three loaves remained: two black, one light. He got them all for a single sketch.

His only real problem came after he'd done two drawings in exchange for a chicken. He was accustomed to poultry wrapped in neat packages, ready for the pan, but this chicken was alive and squawking. He recoiled at the thought of killing it.

He shook his head. "No, I can't take it like this."

The poulterer looked puzzled. "Ya don't know how to kill it?"

"Well . . . it's not the killing. It's . . . it's the, uh, feathers. I can't touch feathers," said Jason, grabbing at the only excuse that came to him. "They give me . . ." and he feigned a seizure, a wild sort of contortion. "You understand?"

The poulterer frowned and looked at his wife. "Feathers?" he said. She snickered.

In the end, Jason received a chicken, dead and plucked, plus five eggs. But he had to pay with three more sketches: the poulterer, his wife, and their son.

Jason was particularly pleased with his sketch of the poulterer. He didn't just draw a face and shoulders. Instead, he portrayed the man working at his trade, as he thought Bruegel might have done. The final picture showed a peasant, stout and bald, chasing a skinny chicken.

By four o'clock, Jason's baskets were filled to overflowing. He had the chicken and eggs, smoked herring, a discarded clamshell, a small pot of mustard, three loaves of bread, lettuce and spinach, dried pears, a round of cheese, a chunk of butter, and two cakes of coarse soap. Best of all, he had a green ribbon for Cat to wear in her hair.

And he still had ink and parchment left.

He was happy with his bounty, but drawing with goose quill on parchment had taken longer than expected. His impatience to get back pushed him into a rapid walk. Filth from the street splashed onto his legs, but he didn't care. And at the town limits, he stopped only a moment to gawk at an odd building that half hung over the canal. He caught a whiff and understood: an outhouse. Next to it was a platform where women were washing cups, plates, and clothes. He pictured his mom's maid doing dishes in the toilet. He took a closer look at the canal and saw the bloated body of a dead dog, and miscellaneous garbage and refuse. The sight was sickening.

He didn't even glance at the playground or the oak as he crossed the canal bridge onto the lane. There weren't many pedestrians this late in the afternoon, so he began to trot. The eggs jostled about, even though he had carefully packed them in layers of grass. His pace didn't slacken.

People, fairground, and fields were soon left behind, and Jason moved into the woods to pick his way from marker to marker. He was now in such a hurry that he barely watched for the mastiffs.

When he finally caught sight of the hovel, his breath caught in his throat. The door was wide open. Had Alba's men been here? He yelled Cat's name and ran across the clearing.

He rushed across the threshold. And there she sat on the bed, wide-eyed and alert.

"I thought you had gone home," she said, no smile, only surprise on her face.

"No." He tried to hide the relief that washed over him as he touched her forehead and found it cool as an autumn dawn. "Where's Charles? He was supposed to guard you."

"He did. But I sent him off to hunt his supper."

"And here's supper for us!" Jason said, holding up the baskets, his face beaming.

Now Cat smiled. "I'm so hungry."

"No wonder. You weren't with us for two whole nights and a day."

"That long? And you stayed?" There was a mix of wonder and gratitude in her voice. "You could have started for home."

Jason ignored her words and busied himself unpacking the baskets, spreading his prizes beside her on the bed. When he came to the ribbon, he held it high and said, "For your hair."

She took the ribbon and threaded it through her fingers, looking at him; it was a shy look, one that he had not seen on her face before. He wasn't sure, but he thought she was blushing. "It's been a long time since I've had something so pretty. Thank you," she said.

He felt his face grow hot. He looked down and began to babble about his escapades in town and his meeting with Griet and their plans for an escape to Paris. His composure was well restored by the time he said, "I know about your father. I'm sorry—I shouldn't have made a fire."

"I must get used to seeing fire," she said. "Winters will be very cold if I don't." She tried to laugh.

"Just the same, I'll cook outside. For you, some chicken broth."

"I'd rather have chicken and bread," she pleaded. "I'm hungry!"

Now he knew she was better, and he searched his memory for ways to cook chicken. Of all the hundreds and hundreds of books he had read, he had managed to skim only a few cookbooks. That had been a must when his mom didn't come home on the cook's night off.

"I'm hungry," she said again, then sank back onto the mattress, slipping into a peaceful nap with the ribbon still laced through her fingers. Jason took the clamshell outside and tossed it into the trees. No need for that now.

He grabbed the shovel and started to dig a fire pit. With Cat on the mend, Jason realized he was once again free to think about Karen. He conjured up her face in his thoughts, but the vision vanished when a chicken recipe popped into his mind. He'd stuff the chicken with bread and spinach and cheese, then roast it on a spit. Cat would like that.

Chapter Eighteen

When the flames faded to red-hot embers, Jason began rotating the chicken on a spit crafted from a green sapling. Above the sizzle of dripping juices, he heard the hovel door creak. Cat, still pale and disheveled, stood in the doorway. Clothes taken from the wooden pegs were slung over her shoulders.

"Off for a bath," she said, waving soap that Jason had bought at market.

"In that little stream?" He thought of the narrow rush of water where he had washed the turnips.

"Where else?" she said and laughed.

He watched her disappear through the bushes at the clearing's edge. Within seconds, Charles bounded in from his hunt, drooled on Jason, sniffed the chicken, cocked his head, and trotted through the bushes after Cat.

Laughter soon floated back to Jason, and he knew the two were splashing in the stream.

When Cat appeared again, Jason had a difficult time reconciling her with the wild and crazy girl he had followed through the woods. She glided toward him in the sedate clothes of her century.

She still wore her long-sleeved shift of cream-colored wool, but now the top half served as a blouse. Over it, she wore a light-blue bodice that laced up the front, and her gray skirt reached nearly to her ankles.

Only a tendril or two of auburn hair showed beneath her white cap. Jason preferred her hair loose or in a single thick braid, but he didn't comment. She had tied the green ribbon around her throat.

He started to speak, "You look . . .You look . . ."

Cat broke in. "Clean? Lovely? Like a lady? Tell me, how do I look?" She fanned out her skirt and did a curtsy.

"Lovely, by all means." He reached out to take her hand, but Charles pushed between them and shook water from his fur.

"Charles! Naughty." Cat smoothed the dog's coat while Jason backed away.

He poked at the chicken—harder than necessary—to test if it was done. "Time for you to eat, my lady," he announced.

Supper started off with Cat sampling a smidgen of everything and exclaiming "oooh" or "ahhh" after each selection. Then she perched on the stool as Jason sat cross-legged on the floor, the trestle table between them. They devoured chunks of buttered bread, lettuce, and half the stuffed chicken, throwing a few tidbits to Charles even though he had found his own supper in the woods.

When they finished, Jason brought out a bowl of dried pears. Cat took one but only toyed with it.

"Cat, why is Alba after you?" Jason asked.

She stared past him as though he weren't there.

"Why?" Jason's tone sharpened.

"Because Alba thinks I have a certain list."

Danger signals rang inside Jason's head. "What list?"

"It's all so confusing and horrible," she said, sharing her pear with Charles.

"I'm waiting."

"Alba knows who most of the Beggars are. That's no secret. They're noblemen." She propped her elbows on the table and rested her chin in her hands. "For months, they've peacefully protested against Spain's tyranny. The religious persecution here has been terrible. So far, thank the Lord, the Beggars have escaped the beheading block." Cat stopped, her eyes looking directly into Jason's. "At first, Alba had no idea that Papa was a Beggar, too, and that his money, lots of it, went to the Beggar cause."

"Griet already told me some of this." Jason stretched out his legs and leaned closer to Cat.

"Strange, isn't it? Noblemen may be noble, but they aren't always rich," she said. "And the time may soon come when these noble Beggars need to buy arms and pay soldiers to fight against Spain's oppression. That's where Papa helped. He gave them plenty of money. And he got his rich friends to do the same. There were ten of them. They all hate Spain's tyranny, and they all want the Beggars to mount a revolt."

"The list, Cat. What about the list?" Jason asked.

Her look told him to be patient. "These men were all acquainted with each other, but they weren't close friends. For that reason, they didn't necessarily trust each other to the fullest."

"You mean there was a chance that one might betray the group to Alba?" *What a risky mess*, Jason thought.

"Unlikely—but yet, a possibility," Cat said. "To prevent betrayal, they vowed loyalty to the Beggar cause and signed their names to a pledge. That way, each would think twice before tattling to Alba. After all, his own name would be on that incriminating list."

"Stupid!" The word burst from Jason's mouth. "They were signing their death warrant—if Alba got hold of the list."

"That's what Papa tried to tell them. But they signed

away. So, Papa signed, too. All wanted to help the Beggars but were afraid to totally trust each other."

"And Alba found out about the list's existence. Right?"

"Sadly, yes. I'm sure it wasn't hard," she said. "Alba has spies everywhere. Papa told me about the list. Other signers probably confided in wives or lovers or friends. Any one of them could have had a slip of the tongue when an Alba spy was on hand to hear."

Cat got up from the stool and pushed it toward Jason. He took it, gratefully, because the hovel floor felt damp. She now sat on the bed, her feet tucked beneath her. Charles rested his head on her lap.

"When Papa went to prison for heresy, Alba had him tortured to find out where the list was hidden." Cat buried her face in Charles's fur, so Jason couldn't tell if she were crying or not.

He reached out and touched her shoulder. "Cat, you told me Alba didn't even know your father was a Beggar."

She raised her head, her eyes free of tears. "Not at first. But once Alba knew about the list, the connection to Papa was plain to see. Papa had denounced the Catholic Church, he followed Luther's teachings, he supported the Calvinists and Baptists, he hated Spain, he was wealthy, and he had good friends—very good friends—among the Beggars. Anyone with half a brain could make the connection."

Cat's voice melted to a hush. "And I'm the next obvious connection."

"Maybe not," Jason said, trying to sound hopeful.

Cat shook her head. "At the burning, I couldn't bear it. Flames were all around Papa. I wanted to comfort him. I wanted him to go to his Maker knowing that Alba would never find the list, that no one else would be caught. I called out to him . . ." She stopped and bit her lip.

"What did you say, Cat?"

Her lip started to bleed. "'I'll destroy it for you, Papa. I promise.'"

Jason went rigid.

Cat's head was now bowed, and she mumbled, "Papa's last words to me were: 'Hush daughter, hush. Run!' And I realized what I had done. I ran."

Chapter Nineteen

Jason couldn't shake the vision of Cat trying to comfort her father while the flames climbed upward. For a time he said nothing, asked nothing, simply sat with her in silence.

When darkness crept into the hovel, she got up and took a candle from the wooden chest, handing it to Jason who ignited it from the embers in the outdoor fire pit.

In the feeble candlelight, they resettled themselves side by side on the bed with Charles resting his head first on one lap, then the other. Finally, Jason asked, "The list. Where is it?"

"In the hatmaker's house. That's why I went there, to destroy it. That house belonged to Papa." Cat scraped a piece of chicken from a bone and gave it to Charles, then scratched behind the dog's ears until his eyes closed.

"The men always met in that house," she said. "Papa bought it just for that purpose. But from time to time, he'd do a little wool trading there; you know, to make things appear normal."

She turned to look squarely at Jason, and her voice rose. "The hatmaker took over the house after Papa died. He simply moved in as if he owned it."

A scowl betrayed her view of the hatmaker, a vulture

with no right to the spoils. But the scowl faded quickly because Charles, deep in his dog dreams, started to snore. Cat laughed. So did Jason, aware that he was now quite attached to this clown of a canine.

"Papa never let me go to that house," she said. "Or even to the town. He didn't want anyone to see me with him. That's why no one knew me when I was caught."

"Griet told me you lived in the country."

Cat stared past the candle into the darkness, and Jason wondered if her thoughts were wandering through rooms she'd never see again. "Yes," she said. "It was a wonderful house. Big and airy. Good for Papa, too, because it wasn't far from the town house, and it wasn't far from his house in Antwerp. Once in a while, I'd stay with Papa in Antwerp, but not often. That house was mostly Papa's place of business."

Cat slipped off her soft-soled shoes and pushed herself back so that she leaned against the hovel wall. Jason did the same. Their shoulders touched. Then Charles squeezed between them, licking Cat's cheek.

"Charles! Get out of here." Jason's voice was stern. The dog looked at him with doleful eyes and slobbered. As Jason wiped away the dribble, his grimace reshaped into a grin. "Ahh, well," he said. Outside, he heard a breeze hum through the branches, and not far off, an owl hooted.

"It was horribly cold when the men came to the town house to sign the pledge," Cat said. "They went upstairs to the great room, and Papa said the ink was almost frozen. But each one listed his name under the pledge. Then they watched while Papa dug out a secret place beneath two bricks in the great room hearth. They hid their treason there."

"I saw the hatmaker's house," Jason said. "Next door to the tavern."

"There's a smithy on the other side. That's why Papa chose that spot. It's a busy place. All sorts of men come and go. They drop by the tavern for tankards of ale, and they go to the smithy to get shoes for their horses or daggers for themselves. No one paid any mind to the men going in and out of Papa's house." Cat kept her gaze downward as she spoke, away from the flickering candle.

Without a word, Jason snuffed out the flame and threw open the shutters. The full moon was huge and bright, like a yellow hole in the sky, pouring golden beams down to the trees, through the branches, and into the hovel.

"Someone living in Papa's house—that gave me a fright when I went there," Cat said. "I expected the place to be empty."

In the moon's mellow light, Jason listened as Cat told what she had done. While the hatmaker chatted with women on the street, she sneaked into the house, through the workroom, up the stairs, into the great room, never knowing where the hatmaker's wife might be, or even if there was a wife. The bricks in the hearth appeared like a puzzle. So many, so alike, so confusing.

"I took too long," Cat said. "When I finally found the right two, I pried them up as fast as I could. I pulled out the money bag first. Dear Papa, he had left the guilders for me." Her gray eyes, now flecked with gold from the moon, filled with tears.

Jason wanted to hold her hand but knew such a gesture would break down their brother-sister pact. So he simply smiled at Cat, and her tears never fell.

"The list was deep down. I couldn't get it out. Then I heard the hatmaker come into his shop and start up the stairs. I pushed the bricks back into place and covered them with ashes.

"But like a fool, I forgot to put the guilders back," she said. "The hatmaker saw me with the sack and screamed that it was his. Who was going to believe me?"

Reliving those moments had visibly drained Cat, and her hand fluttered in an empty gesture. "You know what happened after that," she said. "I was imprisoned."

"It'll happen again, Cat. It's only a matter of time until Alba finds you."

"I know. I told you I'd go to Paris with Griet. And you can go home." For a time, Cat was quiet. Then she said, "But you mustn't tell Griet you're not going with me. I'll tell her at the very last minute. She won't understand why you're deserting your new bride." At that, Cat laughed.

Jason found no humor in the statement, and his face stayed solemn. "I'm to meet Griet in three days. Early in the morning. She warned that you shouldn't go anywhere near town—until the moment you set out for Paris. And then you must be in disguise."

"I understand all that," Cat said. "I'm much safer waiting here."

"Traveling won't be easy," he cautioned. "But you have several days to get strong again. Griet will want to start early on the fourth day, I'm sure." Jason thought that the sooner Cat was away from here, the sooner she'd forget about the list and what might happen to the ten men if Alba got hold of it.

"Will you be ready?" he asked.

"Yes, I'll be ready to go," she said. "After I get the list."

After I get the list! Cat's words sent Jason's heart plummeting. He thought she had given up on the list. He should have known better. He should have guessed that she'd try again. She was determined to get the list or die in the attempt. He didn't argue with her. There was no point. He didn't even murmur a protest. He knew, too, that he'd go with her because he couldn't let her go alone. His decision was as final as hers.

Resigned to it all, he watched as she took off her cap and shook her hair free, then curled up like a cat to sleep the night through.

Chapter Twenty

Jason woke up wishing for a can of Coke and a tube of Crest. *What a lousy century,* he thought.

But he was surprised that he had slept so well on the hard dirt floor, considering that Charles had used his stomach for a pillow much of the night.

He yawned, stood up, stretched, and looked for Cat. She was sitting outside on the ground with the dog. Arranged beside her on a wooden plate were chunks of bread, cheese, and a few dried pears.

"I thought you might need to break your fast," she said. "Last night's supper was a long time ago. Are you hungry?"

"Famished." He waited for Cat to take her food first. When she didn't, he said, "Go ahead."

"I don't usually eat in the morning. Children sometimes grab a piece of bread but rarely adults."

"Then why did you put all this out?"

"I thought you'd be hungry."

"Here," he said, handing her a cheese sandwich. "Eat it. You're too thin."

She laughed and broke off morsels of bread.

Cat was wearing the same clothes as last night but had discarded her stockings and cap. Her hair, now a mass of curls that hung below her shoulders, was held back from her face by the green ribbon.

She gave Jason a pear. With a sly smile, she teased, "Will you marry Karen someday, too, when you get home?"

He choked. How did she know Karen's name?

"Is she really as beautiful as you say?" Cat asked with a light flutter of her eyelashes. "So very, very beautiful? Like a princess?"

"Now wait just one minute," said Jason.

But Cat didn't wait. "You told me so many things. I believed some of them, what you said about Karen and your mother and your father. But most of the things I didn't believe. Yet they were wonderful. You have a gift for telling tales, Jason." Cat's expression turned serious. "They kept me from slipping away. I wouldn't let go because I wanted to hear more." She looked down at her hands, taking time to phrase her words. "For the second time, you've saved my life."

"I didn't know you could hear me."

"Hear, yes," she said. "I just couldn't speak."

"You really had me scared." Jason debated whether to go on. When he made up his mind to continue, his voice was much lower. "I thought you might be dying."

"It was so strange," she said. "I felt a pull from Papa. But I didn't want to go to him because you were telling me such wonderful things."

Jason thought back to those hours by her bedside, how he had talked and talked because he was so homesick, so afraid. Yet now he realized that he had wanted Cat to hear every word. He had wanted to share his faraway life with her.

"Those weren't made-up tales," he said.

Her gray eyes widened.

"You must listen to me," he said. "You probably won't believe me. I won't blame you if you don't."

And he told Cat everything. He thought the telling would be difficult, but it wasn't. It was all straightforward, with none of the verbal hedging and squirming he often did with Karen and his parents.

"I'm not sure I can get home again from the playground. Not sure at all. But I've got to try. Soon," he said.

When he finished, Cat said nothing. Jason wished she would scream and carry on like girls he knew or at least tell him that he was insane to think that he had bridged time and space. But she did none of these things.

"Do you believe me?"

"I don't know," she replied. "If we go to the place of the mud pies and you vanish, then I guess I'll believe you. If we go there and you go nowhere, then I'll know you're a fraud and a liar."

Jason let out a loud guffaw. *Good old Cat calls it like it is,* he thought.

"But I'll be grateful for even a fraud and a liar if he helps me get the list."

"Done," said Jason.

A wide smile crossed her face.

"We should go at night," Jason said.

"No," she countered. "We'd never get in. After dark, doors are bolted from inside. So are shutters. Besides, there's a law in every village Book of Ordinances: Anyone out after dark must carry a lantern. We'd attract too much attention with a lantern, and without one, we'd be challenged—and probably questioned. Someone might even set off a hue and cry." Cat looked at him, shaking her head. "You don't even know what that is, do you?"

"No. But I'd guess it's the sixteenth century's siren."

"Siren?"

"Forget it," he said and patted her hand.

"Well, the hue and cry is terrible," she said. "Someone calls out 'thief' or 'murderer,' and everyone within earshot is supposed to pursue the suspect. The chases can get wild. And if the suspect is caught, he's sometimes beaten to a bloody mess."

"Like I said, we'll not go at night." Jason made a silly face that set off Cat's laughter.

They spent the next few hours sitting in the sun, devising a plan. It was this: Jason would draw a crowd outside the hatmaker's house. And while he distracted the hatmaker and onlookers with sketching and chatter, Cat would sneak inside, go upstairs, retrieve the pledge and list, then scoot out again, unnoticed. It all sounded so simple. But Jason knew it wouldn't be. He was especially unhappy that Cat carried the lion's share of danger, but he had no better alternative; neither did she. He also didn't like the plan because it meant cutting Cat's hair.

Before the morning was over, Cat's auburn hair lay scattered over the ground, raggedly shorn by Jason with the hermit's primitive scissors. She now had a mass of ringlets tight to her head.

Cat then busied herself with altering the hermit's other tunic, which she would wear when they went to town, and from the leftover fabric, she stitched a boy's cap that sat jauntily on her head. Last of all, she mended the rip in her woolen shift.

Jason studied her new look and ran his hand through her short curls. "I don't know. I'm not sure this is going to work."

"It will," she said. "Let's not even think about it until the time comes."

"Agreed." Jason forced himself to appear positive. "We'll just play until I see Griet. Then we'll be on our way—you to Paris; me to my time."

"And we won't worry 'til then," she said firmly.

So that's the way it was: a time of leisure with cares buried and forgotten. Almost.

Chapter Twenty-One

The hours fled into nowhere. All that afternoon and the next day, Cat and Jason blew away the minutes with little thought for the trials ahead.

They fished in the stream with lines of twisted thread, pins, and fat, wiggling worms. But they caught nothing, and neither cared. Both splashed and talked too much to be anglers.

Jason told Cat everything he could think of about his distant century, from astronauts to zoos and more. She never seemed to tire of listening. He taught her, too, how to tell time with his watch and how to dance to rock, substituting his own "dum-dee-bah-bahs" for the blasts of the missing music.

Not once did he mention Karen.

"Where did you learn your Flemish?" she asked. "It's almost perfect."

"I didn't. When I got here, I just knew it. I didn't even know what language it was." Then Jason stopped talking and prompted Cat to tell about herself. He learned that she spoke not only Flemish but French, Italian, and some Latin as well. She knew English, too, but when she spoke it, he could barely make out what she was saying because the pronunciation and grammar were so different from modern English.

He shook his head. "That's not the way I speak it." Then he let out a barrage of modern English.

"Ohhh," she said. "That's English?"

"That's it. Spoken that way every day."

"Do you suppose if I went to your century, I'd speak English as you do?" she asked.

The question threw Jason, and he didn't reply. What did she mean by that? Did she really believe he came from the future? Did she want to go there?

Silence, solid as a wall, separated them.

Finally Cat ventured into the lull. She pointed to a stain on Jason's tunic. "You know, I can take this spot out with heat—and pee," she said, then gave a little giggle.

The way she said it made Jason laugh. He knew she was trying to return to the comfort zone that had existed between them a few minutes before. He helped her. "And, my dear lady, just what other domestic talents do you possess?"

"Griet taught me everything!" Cat told him she could sew, do embroidery, get rid of fleas in the bed and flies in the kitchen, tend a garden, manage servants, and make excellent broth from ox jowls and a tasty stew from eel and herbs. When Jason quizzed her about other foods, he discovered she had never heard of potatoes or pasta, coffee or tea. But when he mentioned ice cream sundaes, she clapped her hands. "Oh Papa and I had some frozen cream in Italy. Is that your ice cream sundae?"

"Not exactly," Jason said. "But close. Our ice cream is cold as snow and smooth as butter. One Sunday afternoon, someone mashed up berries and poured them on top. And so, the ice cream sundae was first served on Sunday."

Cat giggled again. "I'd like to eat one." Then she looked down, a small confession on her lips. "I really don't cook well. But I'm a good weaver. From Papa's weavers, I learned to spin, dye, and weave. Papa didn't want me to be illiterate, either." So, since the age of four, Cat had been tutored in the studies of the day: reading, writing, spelling, composition, literature, and numbers.

Master Eijngaard had also taught her to swim well enough to keep from drowning and to saddle and bridle a horse, ride astride, and not complain.

And somewhere in her fifteen years, Cat had learned to laugh, even when trapped in the worst of life's crises. Jason liked this most of all.

When the two finally tired of talking, they played checkers. Jason scratched squares on the tabletop while Cat collected pebbles, light and dark. "I used to play all the time with Papa," Cat said when she won her fourth game in a row.

On their second day, Jason, still wearing the hermit's tunic, washed his going-home clothes in the stream, smoothing out the wrinkles as they dried. He also managed to shave off his stubble with the hermit's knife, which he sharpened on a rock. It didn't bother him that Cat watched his every stroke.

That night the two sat outside, finding constellations and counting stars in a sky that seemed to stay the same through the centuries. As Jason looked upward, he realized that he didn't even know what the date was. "What year is it?"

"Fifteen sixty-eight," she said. "And what year do you say you come from?"

"Two thousand and three."

She wrote the numbers in the dirt with a stick. "Four hundred and thirty-five years!" She frowned. "Tell me, Jason, you say you live in the year two thousand and three. Then how do you know Pieter Bruegel, who lives now?"

"I didn't say I knew him," he said, ruffling her hair. "I asked you if you knew him. I know only Bruegel's paintings.

They're hanging in lots of special places in two thousand and three."

"His paintings will last that long?"

"Uh-huh," Jason said. "I told you Bruegel was going to be famous. And he is, in my time."

"I'll be gone. Griet and Bruegel and Alba and all of us here will be gone to the beyond. Like Papa's gone. But Bruegel's paintings will still be here. That's hard to imagine, isn't it?"

Jason nodded and took her hand. Together, they strolled around the clearing while crickets chorused in the woods. Charles followed behind them.

"I won't be away long tomorrow," Jason said. "I'll find out final plans from Griet, then hurry back. She wants to get an extra donkey somewhere and make sure the cart's wheels are in good shape."

Jason opened the hovel door, and they went inside to sit in the darkness. "I hate to leave you here alone. But Griet made me promise—you aren't to come near town until she has everything ready. I don't like it, though."

"She's right," Cat said. "I shouldn't show my face any more than need be. Going to the hatmaker's will be bad enough."

Jason hesitated, then he said, almost in a whisper, "Cat, forget the list. If you do, there'll be nearly no danger at all." He couldn't see her face because it was too dark, but he felt a chill invade the room. "All right. Forget I said that."

"Forgotten." She touched his hand.

Jason heard her yawn as she settled on the bed. And he stretched out on the hovel floor with Charles's head once again on his stomach. From Cat came the sound of peaceful breathing. But for him, it was a fretful night.

At dawn on the third day, clouds floated over the land like tattered shrouds, hanging heavy and gray, spreading their gloom. The melancholy morning had no effect on Cat. She chattered and smiled as she accompanied Jason across the clearing and a short way into the woods, Charles at their heels.

Jason wished he could share her optimism. He was still uneasy about leaving her alone. On his previous trek to town, Alba seemed to be only a ghost in Cat's mind. Now, Jason knew Alba was real. "This isn't right, Cat. I shouldn't leave you."

But she would hear none of his protests, sweeping them away like cobwebs. "I'll be fine. Remember, I lived here before—all alone.

"Tell Griet I'm well and ready." She stopped walking and faced Jason. "We'll leave just as we planned. We'll get the list tomorrow morning. By afternoon, I'll be on my way to France with Griet. And you'll be home." For a second, Cat paused, then she came close to speak right into his ear. "Or, you'll be a fool standing amid the mud pies, and it'll be my turn to rescue you."

He tried to smile but couldn't. He knew what she said could well be true. He may never get home. He so desperately wanted to believe that a two-way passage connected his century with hers. But what if it was just a one-way road—to the sixteenth century with no return? He felt numb.

"Don't you dare tell Griet about the list. Or that you're not going to Paris with me," Cat cautioned. "Griet gets angry when a husband deserts. She just may put a hex on you." Her tone was too serious for Jason's liking.

Cat stooped down and plucked a scrap of white paper from a bush. She held it under Jason's nose. With her other hand she playfully poked him in the ribs. "You didn't think I saw you dropping these, did you?"

"I thought I'd get lost," he admitted, somewhat sheepishly.

"Bosh," she said and gave him a gentle shove down the path.

"I'll be back before noon." His voice trailed over his shoulder as he trotted through the trees.

Later, he'd remember Cat as she was that morning. Happy and smiling.

Chapter Twenty-Two

The sensation came to him without warning: a prickle across the back of his neck. He couldn't shake it. He looked at Griet. "I've got to get back to Cat."

The two were standing outside her brother's house. It was a thatched-roof dwelling, a tidy place with two donkeys tethered in the yard, a cart ready for the journey, and clucking chickens carrying out their pick-and-peck existence. Tranquil as the setting was, it did nothing to soothe Jason.

All the way to Griet's he had assured himself that Cat would be safe. Charles was with her, and she'd be all right. But now he knew she wasn't. She was in danger. He could sense it as strongly as if she had called to him.

Griet gestured toward the field. "Go," she said. "I'll see you tomorrow. Both of you. We'll leave then."

Jason gripped her hands in his, then turned to stride swiftly away. He crossed over the main lane, ignoring the canal off to his left and the place of the mud pies beyond it. To save time, he cut diagonally across the field instead of walking along its edge. He kept his head down and his gait steady so he wouldn't attract attention. But halfway across the field, he started to run, eyeing the spot where he'd enter the woods.

He no longer relied on the white markers; the way was almost second nature to him now, and fear of the mastiffs never entered his mind because his every thought centered on Cat. He fought his way along the brambled path and cursed the wooden clogs that slowed his progress, but bare feet would have hindered him even more.

Branches slapped at his face and grabbed at his robe, holding him back like giant fingers. With each step, he berated himself for having left Cat alone. By the time he broke out of the woods into the clearing, his breath had shortened to gasps.

He saw Cat sitting outside the hovel, her legs drawn up, her head resting on her knees. He could see that her bodice was ripped.

"Oh Cat," he cried, his words swallowed by the moan that came from deep inside him. He ran to her.

She looked up, still sobbing. Tears streaked her face.

He threw his arms around her, holding her close. She was trembling.

"Alba's henchman. He found me, Jason."

Jason looked around. "Is he gone?"

"He's gone. Gone," she said, her voice broken with sobs. "He won't bother me again. I was so afraid of the torture, Jason."

"It's all right, Cat. It's all right. You did what you had to." Jason's heart bled for her. He knew she'd hate herself tomorrow and the day after and forever for telling. *But I would have told, too, Cat,* he thought. *Some people can withstand torture. Some can't.* Right then, Jason didn't care who knew where the list was. Or who got caught because of it. He was just grateful that the torturer had let Cat live after she confessed.

He stroked her head and noticed that the front of her hair was singed, that her face was flushed. His hands moved up and down her arms, testing for injuries. Then he tried to pull together her bodice, which had been ripped apart.

That's when he saw bloodstains on her shift. With his sleeve, he wiped away a smear of blood from her neck.

"He had a knife," she said.

"Are there other cuts?"

She shook her head.

Jason didn't want to ask, but he wanted to know. "Did he . . ."

Cat didn't let him finish. "No, he didn't rape me. The soldiers do that. He was a torturer."

For a long time, they sat together in silence, Jason rocking Cat back and forth and rubbing his hand over her back. Finally, he asked, "Can you tell me?"

She pulled away from his embrace and sat up straight. "Yes," she said. "I want to. Right after you left, I came back here. I swept up and made the bed."

Jason took hold of her hand and held it between both of his.

"I knew I wouldn't be living here any longer, but I needed to plant more seeds; you know, for anyone else who might come along and live here. Charles came with me. But he kept digging holes and scattering seeds, so I shooed him into the forest to play.

"After I finished planting, I came inside to pack." She stopped, her attention drawn by an ant that crawled hurriedly across her skirt. When it disappeared into the grass, she glanced up at Jason and spoke, her voice filled with melancholy. "It had started as such a good morning, Jason. I kept wondering about you and Griet, how you were getting on together.

"I spread my red coverlet on the floor and loaded it with needle, thread, soap, bread, cheese, whatever else I thought might come in handy on the journey. I took Papa's wooden bowl, too, his Beggar bowl.

"Then I rolled it all into a bundle and was just tying it together with my stockings when I heard the door creak. I didn't turn," Cat said, shrugging her shoulders. "There was no need to turn. Charles always pushes open the door with his nose after a run in the woods. He likes to drop down on the cool dirt floor. But this morning, I didn't hear him snuffling. . . ."

Jason watched terror creep into Cat's eyes.

"When I turned," she said, "Charles wasn't there. A man was there, standing in the doorway. A Spaniard, and I knew he was one of Alba's.

"He was a big man, Jason. Not as big as you, but big. His dark hair was cut close to his head, and his moustache and beard were well trimmed. He was smiling. An evil smile."

Chapter Twenty-Three

"He just stood there in the doorway, and he hissed 'The list. I'll take the list now.'"

Cat smoothed her skirt over her knees, then twisted her forefinger in the fabric. She didn't talk but kept twisting.

"Go on, Cat," Jason said.

"He said his name was Luis Javier de Toledo and that he was Alba's special confidant and torturer.

"I tried to tell him I didn't know anything about a list, but he didn't believe me."

Jason lightly touched Cat's neck where the blood had dried. He could see a purple bruise forming around the cut.

"No one was with him," she said and again placed her hand in Jason's. "I picked up my bundle to throw it at him. But I stopped when I saw his dagger."

Jason could imagine Cat's fear. There was nowhere for her to run. No one to help her.

"He shoved me to the ground. Then he put the dagger at my neck. I didn't move. I didn't even breathe. He made just a small cut. I could tell that it angered him when I didn't cry out.

"He said he'd been searching for me for weeks. He'd seen me at the burning, weeping and calling to Papa. But I disappeared in the crowd. He was sure Papa had given me the list, and he started to hunt for me. He finally found me at the gallows."

Jason thought back to their flight across the field. "It was the Spaniard who followed us, wasn't it? He lost us in the rain. Then he searched again in the morning, didn't he?"

"Yes. The mastiffs caught his scent. He was furious, Jason. The dogs treed him, and he blamed us."

Cat's words flowed faster now, mixing with a single bird's trill that wafted through the tree tops. Jason couldn't reconcile the lilting notes with the horrors he was hearing. The Spaniard had kicked Cat, then stood over her, placing his boot on her stomach. He grabbed her wrists and bound them with leather thongs. He tied her ankles; then, with practiced ease, he strung her up to the hovel's crossbeam, her feet only inches from the floor.

With one hand, Jason gently pushed back the sleeves of Cat's shift to look at her wrists. Red rings from the rope still showed.

"He slapped me and pushed his face close to mine. His breath was hot." Cat grimaced, a shudder racing through her body. "I'll never forget his words. He spit them at me: 'I have no problem with maiming,' he hissed. 'Or killing. Actually, that's what I do best. I prefer it to planting peas and beans like the peasants.' Then he laughed. It was the devil's laugh, Jason."

The Spaniard's brutality seared through Jason's thoughts, making his body tense. He didn't realize he was squeezing Cat's hand too tightly until she moved her fingers. He loosened his grip.

"I was so scared, Jason," she said. "I didn't know what he'd do to me. I was afraid I'd tell where the list was hidden. I knew you wouldn't be back soon, so I started to scream for Charles. I screamed and I screamed. To shut me up, he stuffed the hermit's cap in my mouth."

For a brief moment, Cat closed her eyes. When she opened them, she faced Jason. "You know what?" she said with the smallest of smiles. "The Spaniard thought you were Charles. He thought I was calling for you. He told me I needn't bother because he had seen you going to market."

Right then, Jason truly hated himself. He should have known they were being watched. And he should never have left Cat alone. "I'm so sorry for leaving you," he said.

"You couldn't have known the Spaniard would find us, that he'd come here. Neither of us could have known that. We seemed so safe."

A soft look came to her eyes. "I want you to know something, Jason. I think it was so noble of you to have traded your ring and gold band to Father Francis. We couldn't have eaten otherwise."

Jason didn't understand why she was saying this. Not now, anyway. Then Cat continued, and he knew.

She spoke quickly, her voice almost inaudible as though she didn't want Jason to hear this part of her tale. She told how the Spaniard had waved both ring and watchband in front of her nose. Father Francis had given them to him—for a price, of course—along with the news that a strange young man was now in town. "de Toledo guessed that you were my bridegroom. He thought it amusing that you had approached a priest. So many priests are loyal to Alba. But you couldn't have known that, Jason."

He groaned. "My watchband and ring! That's how the Spaniard figured out we were still in the area, isn't it? Then he just had to watch the woods until one of us came out to go to town." Jason's hand flew to his forehead, hitting it hard. "And my markers led him straight to you!"

"He would have found us anyway—markers or no markers," she said.

But her words failed to ease Jason's conscience. Guilt overpowered him.

"de Toledo kept harping about the list, over and over and over again while he paced around me," she said.

Cat bit her lower lip. She seemed reluctant to go on. When she finally spoke again, her words came haltingly. "He told me he'd let me live . . . if I told . . . or I'd die slowly if I didn't. It was up to me. All I had to do was tell where the list was hidden." Cat stopped. She shook her head. "I prayed that I could withstand the tortures he intended to use. He took the gag out of my mouth so I could answer him. Instead I screamed for Charles."

Cat stared blankly into space, as though mesmerized by her next memory. The Spaniard had gone to the fire ring. Within minutes, flames flared and crackled.

"I didn't turn my head, Jason. I looked straight at the fire. I remembered Papa burning, but I didn't look away."

Jason wiped away the tears as Cat talked on. The Spaniard had thrust his dagger blade deep into the red-hot embers and waited until the metal shimmered with heat. Then with gloved hand, he retrieved his weapon.

"He walked toward me. Slowly, so I'd have time to think about what he was going to do. He smiled when he lifted my skirt. Then he pressed the blade against my leg. Oh, Jason, I could smell my flesh burning. I fainted."

Jason didn't know how much more of this he could stand. He gently lifted Cat's skirt and saw the ugly burn that slashed along the lower portion of her leg. Jason started to get up.

"No. Let me finish. I want to get over this—and then I want never to speak of it again." Cat took hold of Jason's arm and pulled him down to sit beside her.

"I don't know how long I was unconscious. Maybe only seconds. But when I came to, the Spaniard was back at the fire. And I started screaming louder for Charles."

Cat slowly described how her torturer had crouched down to blow on the flames. Once again, he buried the dagger in the glowing embers. As he waited, he repeated his threats, this time with anger fueling his words.

"He came over and cut me down," she said. "Then he clutched my bodice and dragged me to the fire. I kicked and yelled but couldn't get free. He was much too strong. He threw me onto the ground with my head close to the fire and put his foot on my back."

Jason touched her singed curls, then trailed his fingers along her flushed cheeks.

"I'll never forget what he said then: 'I've no time to play with you. We'll make this quick. You have such a pretty face, but not for long. You'll be blind, too, once I push your face into the fire.'

"He shoved my face closer and closer. I screamed and screamed."

"Stop it, Cat. Stop it. That's enough. You'll make yourself sick. No one could have withstood that. And no one will blame you for telling. No one. Ever."

Cat jerked away from him. "You think I told?"

Jason stared at her in confusion. "Well, yes. Your face isn't burned. And de Toledo is gone."

"He *is* gone. Like Papa is gone. And like we'll all be gone someday. Griet and Bruegel and you and I. And may God have mercy on the Spaniard because his sins on earth were many."

"He's dead?" Jason could barely comprehend what was being said to him.

Cat got up and pulled Jason to the hovel door. She pushed it open. And he looked in.

The scene told its own story. Charles stood guard over the Spaniard's body, the throat ripped open, blood still seeping onto the dirt floor.

"de Toledo never even heard Charles," she said. "He never growled, never made a sound. He just crawled closer and closer. Then he lunged."

"Good dog, Charles," Jason whispered.

Chapter Twenty-Four

Jason pressed Cat's face between his hands, kissed her on the forehead, and hugged her. Then he hugged Charles, scratching behind the dog's ears, patting his head, and praising him for saving Cat.

"It's all right, Charles," he said. "It's all right." He gradually coaxed the dog away from the body.

For a time, all three clung together.

Then while Cat sat on the bed, Jason put a poultice on her leg where the blade had seared a six-inch brand. He bound the burn with strips of his T-shirt, aware that the bandages were far from sterile, but at least they were clean. Cat flinched only once.

"We've got to bury him and get out of here." He made sure his voice sounded steady although his nerves were not. "The Spaniard will be missed. There'll be a search."

"I know," she said.

Jason discovered that he wasn't the least bit squeamish when he reached into the pouch on the dead man's belt to retrieve his ring and watchband. It had been foolish to make that trade with the priest. He had underestimated the danger before; he wouldn't again.

"We can't wait until tomorrow to leave. We'll get the list this afternoon. We can hide with Griet tonight. You can be on your way at dawn." Jason grabbed the corpse by the ankles and dragged it to the door.

"I'll help you dig the grave," Cat offered. "I've done it before."

Jason shook his head and pointed to the hovel floor. "You can cover the bloodstains with dirt. We can't leave any traces."

For once, he was glad not to be in the twenty-first century with all its police techniques. Here, they wouldn't have to worry about Alba or the bailiff finding fingerprints or fibers or microscopic bloodstains. But there was still motive that could place the murder at their doorstep. The Spaniard had been hunting them, and that was a good-enough reason for murder in any century. Eventually—maybe in a day, maybe a week—Father Francis would put it all together.

Jason reattached his watch to the band and noticed that it was nearly noon. He needed to hurry, but as he started out the door with the corpse, Cat put her hand gently on his arm, stopping him.

"We need to wrap the body for burial," she said. "It's only proper."

Exasperated, Jason waited while she looked around the hovel for a suitable shroud. She found nothing: no spare blanket, no cloth, not even fabric from extra clothes. Then her hand touched the mattress on which she sat. "I won't be sleeping here anymore. We'll use this."

They dumped out the dried leaves. Then they stuffed the body into the mattress cover through its open end. Satisfied, Cat gave a wordless signal, sending Jason off to the woods with his burden.

For the gravesite, he found an open spot where Cat's garden spade wouldn't have to hack through big tree roots. The plot was a safe distance from the hovel and near the winding stream. Before Jason had dug down a foot, perspiration beaded his forehead. Another foot and the hermit's tunic would be soaked with sweat, so he took it off and draped it over a bush. He now wore only his shorts and the clumsy clogs.

It didn't take him long to get a rhythm to his digging, and he thought back to when he had first made serious use of a shovel. That was a dozen years ago; he and his Cub Scout buddies had cultivated a little garden in a Chicago vacant lot. But they had neglected to water the seeds, so nothing much grew except straggly weeds.

As he dug, Jason wondered what he would have done if he had returned when the Spaniard was torturing Cat. Would he have killed the man? Yes, he would have. The realization struck him that he was no longer the Parkman High junior of a week ago. In this place and century, decisions were his to make, and he made them, right or wrong. He now had some steel in his backbone, and he was thankful for that.

When he finished digging, it was nearly two o'clock. He rolled the corpse into the pit and covered it with dirt, concerned that scavengers might unearth the body. But he couldn't risk a mound of rocks, a telltale sign of burial. The best he could do was disguise the grave with a scattering of last autumn's leaves. Once the job was done, he took his tunic and headed for the stream.

The setting was idyllic. A dam of logs, sticks, and leaves slowed the stream's flow, creating a small pool no bigger than a bathtub. Jason kicked off his clogs and took off his shorts. Then he slipped into the water to wash away dirt, sweat, and the Spaniard's blood.

Just as he was ready to climb out, he heard Cat say, "You'll be needing these?" He looked up to see her waving his shorts and tunic.

"Cat!" he yelled. "Out of here."

She laughed. Then she tossed his clothes onto a branch near the water's edge. "I'll hide my eyes," she said, grinning.

"You'll do more than that. You'll turn around and face that tree."

Feigning reluctance, she turned until her back was toward him and her nose touched the tree's bark. "Good enough?"

"That'll do." He was happy to see Cat back to her playful self. And he marveled at how she recovered from trauma, or at least pretended to—her days in the town tower, the near hanging, the mastiffs, and the torture. He knew of no one else who could have struggled through those trials and still mustered a laugh. Certainly not his mom, or his dad, or Karen. Or himself.

He climbed out of the pool and shook water from his hair the way a dog does after a swim. Then he brushed excess water from his body, giving no thought to towels. When he finished dressing, he walked up to Cat. "You can take your nose out of the tree now."

"Are you sure? You're all dressed and everything?"

"All together—combed and groomed and ready for town," he said.

Cat did a pirouette. "And how do I look?" She smoothed her hands over the remodeled tunic, then put on the cap that partially covered her auburn curls. "Do I look like a boy?"

Cat could never look like a boy, not with those big gray eyes that mirrored blue and green when the light changed. And not with skin as smooth as vanilla creme. Instead of answering her question, Jason said, "You look great."

She was pleased. Jason was not. What if another of Alba's henchmen recognized her in town? She'd be caught and executed.

"Where is he buried?" she asked. Jason led her through the trees to the grave. She stood for a moment, muttering a brief prayer that Jason couldn't hear and didn't want to hear.

Abruptly, she turned and joined Jason to walk back to the hovel.

When they came to the clearing, Cat picked a blade of grass and blew three signals, followed by three more. Within seconds, Charles bounded out of the woods and stood at her feet, wagging his tail.

Inside the hovel, the afternoon sunlight beamed through the two windows, gilding each dust mote that drifted through the air. The place was peaceful, as though nothing had happened. Jason stooped to examine the spot where the Spaniard had fallen and could find no signs of the morning's violence.

Cat inspected her red-blanket bundle, then tied her clothes together to make another bundle. Jason did the same with his jacket, jeans, shoes, and shirt. They'd hide these by the pond where they'd first bathed, where Cat had snagged her shift and protested that she wasn't a witch. How long ago was that? Jason did a mental count. Less than a week, although it seemed like months, years.

"Charles can stand guard over the bundles while we're in town," Cat said. "He'll stay by the pond if I tell him to." That solution suited Jason because he didn't want Charles trying to follow Cat into the hatmaker's house.

In haste, they wolfed down the last of the food, sharing it with Charles. The room was silent except when the dog licked and chomped. He was overly fond of cheese.

Jason was the first to finish. He took the quill, ink, and parchment from the shelf. "Is there no other way?" he asked, worrying about the dangers ahead for Cat.

She shook her head and brushed a few crumbs from her tunic. "It's mine to do. I know the house, and you don't. I know where the bricks are, and you don't. Anyway, it's my list to get. You'll have enough to do keeping the hatmaker busy."

"Cat, it didn't work for you before. You were caught.

What if it doesn't wo—?" Jason never finished the question because Cat had placed her fingers to his lips.

"Shhhh," she whispered.

They said no more, picked up their bundles, and with Charles at their heels, they walked out of the hovel, closing the door firmly behind them.

Chapter Twenty-Five

Jason stood before the hatmaker's house and looked up and down the street. Where was Cat hiding? Behind the barrels at the tavern? Beside the wagon at the smithy's? She was doing a good job of concealing herself; he couldn't see her anywhere.

He heard a bang behind him and spun around. It was just the door of the public outhouse. He was getting jumpy. If they were caught, Jason knew they'd be put to death at the end of a noose. And if one of Alba's men recognized Cat, she'd be tortured and burned at the stake.

There was only one thing that lifted his spirits: The door of the hatmaker's house stood ajar.

The hatmaker strutted back and forth along his street-side display, straightening brims, smoothing feathers, nodding to passersby, all the while preening and posturing like a potbellied peacock. The hats—there must have been thirty of them—were arranged on wooden shelves affixed to the front of the house.

The hatmaker stopped his pacing to survey his domain, his feet planted far apart. His girth exceeded plumpness, and he rested his hands on his belly. By anyone's standards, he was overstuffed and overdressed. His black doublet had popped some of its ball buttons, leaving a sizeable gap to show what once had been a waistline. Now it was flab. Pudgy legs showed below puffed-out pants of pink and gray, and his triple chins lay in folds on his pleated collar.

Such a pompous fool should be easy prey for flattery. Jason went to work.

He approached the display. "How exquisite! What a masterpiece I could create—you and your chapeaux!" With a flourish, Jason brought out his parchment and quill, assuming an artist's pose. He wiggled his ring finger so the late afternoon light sparkled on the sapphire. A gleam of interest shone in the hatmaker's eye.

Jason offered his hand. "Jason of Antwerp. Perhaps you've seen my paintings? I've studied with the great Pieter Bruegel," he said, appalled that he could lie so easily and so outrageously.

The hatmaker eyed Jason's hand and ring. "The Bruegel whose snow scene hangs in the shop down the street?"

"That's the one. Do let me sketch you with one of your creations." Jason unrolled his parchment. "From my sketches, I will do an oil in the privacy of my studio in Antwerp."

At the mention of "studio" and "Antwerp," the hatmaker's tongue flicked lightly across his lower lip, and his eyes sparkled even brighter.

"It would give me such pleasure to record your genius for posterity," said Jason.

"At what price?"

"Not a penny! My pleasure." Then, fearing he had overdone it a bit, Jason added, "Of course, if you want to bestow one of your hats upon me in return, how could I refuse?"

The hatmaker smiled.

Jason placed his parchment, quill, and ink on an empty corner of the hat shelf. He was now ready to court a crowd. He surveyed the array of hats and picked up a fur-trimmed beret. "Hold this one," he said.

The hatmaker wrinkled up his nose. "No," then he fingered a lady's close-fitting cap decorated with purple ribbon, pink feathers, and teardrop pearls. "This one, I think."

"No, no. Too flamboyant. It will detract from your princely presence." With exaggerated care, Jason looked over the hats, choosing a green one with a lone feather in its crown. "This will do beautifully." He spoke louder now to summon the curious.

"And this one, too?" said the hatmaker. He waved a floppy red wool hat with a shell badge on its crown.

"By all means. And that one." Jason pointed to a black felt hat rounded like a kettle.

"And this one?"

"No, that one!"

"What about this one?"

A crowd gathered as the two quibbled over choices. Soon, onlookers began voicing their own preferences, and before long the street in front of the hatmaker's house resembled the hubbub of a rummage sale, with people picking and shoving and pointing.

When the fussing finally quieted, the hatmaker cradled a half-dozen hats and wore a seventh on his head. He held his multiple chins upward and pulled his belly inward as far as it would go.

Jason began to sketch and made sure to hold the parchment so all could see. The crowd watched, enthralled, as each fresh line appeared.

From the edge of his vision, Jason saw a slim form scoot around the crowd and slip through the hatmaker's front door. No one seemed to notice. But Jason's hand shook.

Chapter Twenty-Six

Not a sheet of parchment remained. Jason's ink was gone, too. And where was Cat?

He had completed four drawings, adding far more detail than usual to drag out the process. With each stroke of the quill, Jason had expected to see Cat sneak out of the house. But she hadn't. Why was she still inside?

Onlookers didn't linger now that the sketching show was over. They went their way, leaving Jason in the company of only the hatmaker. With no crowd to conceal her, Cat would never be able to slip out of the door unnoticed, and Jason didn't know how to help her. He stood, somewhat numbly, watching the house and, beyond it, an orange-red sun that slid lazily below the horizon.

The hatmaker pranced about. He held up the sketch Jason had given him. "You'll use the other sketches to do an oil painting? A finished portrait of me—with my hats?"

"Of course," Jason lied.

"Soon? Remember, no hat for you until it's done," the hatmaker said, shaking his fat finger.

"A week," Jason lied again.

The hatmaker looked impressed. "You must work quickly."

Maybe too quickly, Jason thought. If he had worked slower, he might have held the crowd longer and given Cat more time to escape. What was she doing in there? He needed to find out.

"Here, let me help you," he said to the hatmaker, who was closing shop for the night. Jason scooped up a half-dozen hats and trotted after the hatmaker into the house.

"Put them here." The hatmaker placed his own armful of berets, cloches, and stocking caps on a long wooden table.

Jason walked through a scatter of scraps to do the hatmaker's bidding. Shreds of fabric, bits of ribbon, and ends of thread littered the floor, and strips of fur hung from the ceiling. With one glance, Jason could tell the workshop offered no place for Cat to hide. Supplies sat on open shelves. The lone cabinet was no bigger than a dollhouse. Even Cat, slim as she was, couldn't get in there.

Jason peeked into the room beyond and saw a high desk topped with a ledger, a quill, and ink, and on the floor, a strongbox. Again, no cupboards to hide in, no doors to escape through.

The whole place reeked of cabbage. The smell wafted through the downstairs rooms, souring Jason's stomach. He disliked cabbage even more than turnips.

He was glad to get outside again and relished the clean air. But his respite lasted only a few seconds because the hatmaker now expected his help. Back and forth Jason went, toting the unsold hats to the workroom. With each trip, he plotted how he would get upstairs to look for Cat.

When he had placed the last beret on the inside table, Jason sniffed the air with feigned delight. "Mmmmm, something smells delicious." He unrolled his sketches and held one up. "This for a bit of tasty supper?" he bargained.

"Then you'll have only two left," the hatmaker said. "Can you do my oil with only two sketches to consult?"

"I could do it from memory," Jason bragged. "But I'll keep two—just in case. No detail should be left out."

The hatmaker tittered in delight. His chubby hands clutched the second sketch as he said, "Yes, yes, come to supper."

The invitation had no sooner been uttered than a woman's voice snapped, "Joos, get up here. Soup's ready."

In an instant, the vinegary voice transformed the hatmaker from pompous fool to henpecked husband. "Ahhh, Geertruid, dearest. Yes. Coming. Coming," the hatmaker replied, his words slathered in honey. "I have a surprise."

Under other circumstances, Jason might have risked a smirk, but not now. Instead, he climbed the stairs behind the hatmaker. The steep steps creaked beneath their feet.

From the top of the stairs, Geertruid glowered at them. She was plump and red faced, with a wooden spoon in her hand. "Joos! There's only soup for two!" she shouted.

The hatmaker halted in midstride. Jason, however, refused to be stopped. He reached around the hatmaker's ample girth to tap the drawing. "A promise is a promise," he whispered, giving the hatmaker a prod in the rump.

The hatmaker resumed his climb. Jason followed. Geertruid watched.

Chapter Twenty-Seven

Jason flashed his most winning smile while Geertruid looked him up and down. "Hmmmpf," she grunted from behind lips that seemed sewn shut. As for Joos, he busied himself picking lint from his gray-and-pink pants.

It was an uneasy encounter, at best. The three stood on the second-floor landing that led into the great room in the front half of the house and to the kitchen in the rear.

Geertruid spoke. "Well, introduce us, Joos."

"Ahh, dearest," the hatmaker began. "This is . . . ah . . ." He looked at Jason. "What did you say your . . ."

"Jason, the artist of Antwerp. At your service." Jason stepped forward, ready to kiss the hand of his hostess if required. It wasn't.

"I've never had much use for paint dabblers," Geertruid said and turned her back on Jason before flouncing into the kitchen. "I'll water the soup."

"Oh, let me help you." Jason moved to the kitchen threshold and cast a quick glance inside but saw only the usual clutter of crockery, a washbasin, a wooden tub big enough for bathing, a worktable, a bolted back door—and nowhere to hide.

"Out!" Geertruid ordered. She shook her wooden spoon, spraying droplets of soup through the air. Jason retreated. But no matter, he had seen what he needed to see: Cat wasn't in the kitchen.

"Come," Joos said.

Jason followed the hatmaker across the landing into the great room, which combined sleeping, eating, and living quarters. Against the far wall stood the couple's bed, a fluffy-looking mattress on a platform. At night, curtains could be drawn to enclose the sleepers, but they were open now. Jason could see that Cat wasn't hiding there. A tabby kitten slept on the coverlet, undisturbed by the clattering of pots and pans from the kitchen.

Joos plopped into one of two wooden chairs in front of the fireplace. His whole body relaxed, and he stifled a yawn. "Sit," he said, patting the second chair.

Jason obeyed, only to find that the chair offered no more comfort than a church pew. He gazed into the fireplace where flames licked the bottom of a blackened kettle suspended from a hook. The kettle's contents bubbled, spewing forth the pungent odor of cabbage soup.

It took a moment for Jason to realize that the fireplace was backless so that it served both the great room and the kitchen. How convenient. Geertruid could stir her soup from whichever room she chose. He peered through the flames to see her skirt swishing about the kitchen, first one way, then the other, as she prepared the evening meal. He hoped Cat had witnessed a similar scene. Maybe the sight of Geertruid's oversized feet had warned her in time.

There came a snort, then the easy rhythm of snoring. Joos was napping, his head cushioned on his chest by multiple chins. Jason now felt free to twist around and examine the rest of the room. It was rectangular in shape, lit by candles. A loom stood in one corner and a table set for two in another.

The walls held their share of this and that: Jason saw a dreadful painting of a ship at sea; clothes hanging from hooks; mugs, tongs, and trivets dangling from more hooks; shelves filled with plates and pitchers; and a crossbow over the mantel. He couldn't imagine Joos handling a crossbow. Geertruid, maybe?

Across from the fireplace was the room's only window, made up of small diamond-shaped panes held together with lead. Beneath it sat a long storage chest, the lid serving as a seat.

Jason blinked. He first doubted what he saw. But it was there: an inch of green ribbon sticking out from beneath the lid. Cat's? Or trimming from one of Joos's many hats?

Before Jason could get up to look, Geertruid came into the room. With a scowl, she plunked a third bowl, knife, and spoon onto the table.

Jason manufactured his best grin.

He needed to lift the lid of that chest. But there was no opportunity now because Geertruid lumbered to and from the kitchen, bringing to the table bread and butter, hard-boiled eggs, a bowl of mussels, and a pitcher of ale to round out their meal of cabbage soup.

Jason scanned the room again, thinking, hoping a plan would come to mind. That's when he saw what he had missed before. Two bricks on the hearth sat slightly higher than the rest. He bolted from his chair. Just as he reached the fireplace, Geertruid reappeared carrying a soup tureen. She eyed him suspiciously.

Jason gave her a weak smile and a nervous nod. "Looks delicious," he said and pretended to warm himself by the fire, although he already felt sweat on his brow. "Cabbage soup is my favorite. Why, my mother used to make it every Saturday night. I can tell just by the smell, yours is far better." All the while Jason babbled, his feet were gently working the bricks back into place.

Geertruid poked Joos in the shoulder. "Soup's on. Get to the table."

The three sat down together, and while Geertruid ladled soup from the tureen into their bowls, Jason stole another look at the bench. The ribbon was gone. *Cat is in there,* he thought. *She heard my voice and sent me a signal.* Inwardly, he moaned. She was trapped like a bird in a box, and he didn't know what to do. At least she could breathe because the chest's ill-fitting joints and age-old cracks kept it from being airtight. He turned back to the supper-laden table.

"And what were you gawking at?" Geertruid asked.

"Nothing," Jason said.

Geertruid stared in the direction of the bench, then glared at Jason. He tried to appear calm, even though he had no idea how to rescue Cat from the window bench. And to make matters worse, something with six legs was swimming in his bowl of cabbage soup.

Chapter Twenty-Eight

Jason was determined to swallow the bug on a silent count of three. One, two, three. He spooned it into his mouth, but it wouldn't go down. So, he chewed. Would this supper never end?

Between slurps, Geertruid chided Joos. "Stupid! You wasted precious time getting your picture drawn! You should have been selling hats. That's what you should have been doing."

Joos made no attempt to answer, letting his wife's criticism flow in a steady stream. "What a fool you are to make hats that no one orders. There they sit. Fool!"

Joos sighed.

Jason listened, knowing that poor Joos was actually ahead of his time: He built up an inventory of hats and displayed them, enticing passersby to stop, admire, and eventually buy.

"Why didn't you sell the black cap to the weaver? I saw him trying it on," Geertruid said. "I know why. You were too busy posing for this dabbler."

Joos shrugged a shoulder.

"Tomorrow, put the ladies' hats in front of the berets."

She pushed the saltcellar in front of the mustard to indicate proper placement.

Joos put down his spoon. "I think I know my business," he said to his soup.

"I doubt that," Geertruid replied. "The money box is almost empty."

Joos closed his eyes.

Jason changed the subject. "Lovely house you have."

Joos smiled. "Yes, the man who owned it was bur—, well, he died. And Geertruid thought he'd like us to look after it. Didn't you dearest? So, we moved in."

Geertruid frowned at her husband.

"That's his crossbow up there." Joos pointed toward the mantel.

"Joos! Eat your soup," Geertruid ordered, tapping her spoon on the hatmaker's bowl.

Jason buttered his bread and acknowledged that there was no way he could rescue Cat. Geertruid would always be there, watching him just as she watched Joos.

Cat would have to escape on her own in the black of night when the candles were out, when the firelight was gone, when Geertruid and Joos were sound asleep behind their bed curtain.

Just as Geertruid's mouth—full of mussels and mustard—opened to talk, Jason broke in. He spoke loudly so Cat could hear. "I must leave soon," he said, glancing from his host to his hostess. "I'm sure you go to bed early."

"Yes," said Joos.

"No," said Geertruid.

Jason tried another approach. "It must get cool in here when the fire dies down. I suppose you have to close your bed curtain to keep out the chill." The volume of his voice increased.

"We do, we do," said Joos. "It's a fine piece of fabric that my dearest Geertruid wove. Takes the wear and tear. Isn't that right, my dear?"

Geertruid raised a brow and swallowed ale.

"Speaking of wear and tear, when I climbed those front steps of yours, Joos, I noticed they were pretty creaky. I could fix them for you when I come back with your painting. It would take no time at all." In truth, Jason didn't know a bolt from a nail, but he did know that if Cat used the front stairs, the creaking would certainly wake Geertruid.

"I'd be much obliged to have you fix them." Joos patted Jason's hand.

"Absolutely not," Geertruid said. "The creaks tell me when someone's on the stairs."

"Good point," Jason said. Then he held up a boiled egg before slicing it in half. "Do you keep chickens in the back?"

"Six hens, one rooster," said Joos proudly. "Geertruid gathers eggs every morning, don't you dearest?"

"It must be quite handy to feed them out the back door."

Geertruid's back went rigid. "Young man, I don't like artists, and I don't like strangers who butt in where they're not wanted. You ask too many questions for my pleasure. You have the manners of a bedbug."

"Do forgive me." Jason bowed his head in apology, his nose nearly in his soup.

He resumed eating and hoped with all his heart that Cat had understood his message: Wait until they go to sleep, when their bed curtain will be closed. Don't use the front stairs. Go out the back door, instead.

Further attempts to strike up conversation went nowhere. Geertruid and Joos were too busy wiping bread around their bowls to get up the last bits of cabbage. It was a solemn undertaking, and Jason politely followed suit until not a shred of his cabbage remained.

When they had finished eating, Geertruid and Joos daintily picked their teeth with silver picks. That accomplished, the meal was officially over. Geertruid cleared away the supper dishes and tidied up the kitchen. Joos swept the hearth.

While both were occupied with chores, Jason stood at the window, one clog touching the bench. "Good view you have here," he commented casually as he peered past the open shutters to the street below.

Joos nodded and fed a few clumps of peat to the fire. As the flames gobbled the fuel, Jason gently tapped his clog against the bench. Three taps, a pause, then three more taps—the same sequence Cat had used to summon Charles from the woods.

From within the bench came three faint scratches, then three more.

Geertruid stormed into the room. Jason whirled around, certain that he had been found out.

Then to his disbelief, Geertruid strode past him, straight to Joos. She shook her wooden spoon, this time splattering droplets of soapy water in the air. "I told you to set the traps for those rats! They're getting bold as bears," she yelled. "Are you deaf? Didn't you hear?"

"Yes, dearest," the hatmaker said. "Did you see one?"

Joos winced while Jason drew a deep breath and silently blessed the rats of the sixteenth century.

Chapter Twenty-Nine

Jason left the hatmaker's house. Behind him, the door clicked shut, and the bolt was rammed into place. On the street, not a soul was in sight.

He couldn't bear to think of Cat cramped inside the wooden chest while Joos puttered about, doing nothing, and Geertruid stitched away at needlepoint, her tongue tossing barbs at will. When would they go to bed?

He reached under his tunic to get his watch, which was tied to his shorts. He slipped the band over his wrist and read the luminous dial. Eight o'clock.

Off-key singing drifted from the tavern next door, but Jason heard no shouts from the town crier. He remembered well Cat's warning that anyone without a lantern would be challenged by the crier.

His first impulse was to wait for Cat in the passageway that threaded between the hatmaker's house and the smithy's next door. She'd have to come through there if she slipped out the back door. But what if she came out the front? He needed to keep that in view, too.

He scanned the street for a hiding place, rejecting the barrels outside the tavern and the wagon beside the smithy's. They gave too little cover.

There was only one sanctuary: the public outhouse. A shabby shack, it stood directly across from the hatmaker's house and half hung over the canal. The prospect of hiding there revolted Jason, but he ran to it, pushed open the door, and stepped inside. The stench smacked him on the nose.

His cabbage soup rose to his throat, but he kept it down. Every smell from the canal below—sewage; garbage; dead dogs, cats, and rats—funneled upward into the outhouse. Unable to dissipate into the open air, the stench stayed bottled up within the structure's wooden walls.

The quarters were close with room for only one, and Jason pushed the bolt, locking himself inside. He hoped no ale drinkers from the tavern needed an outhouse tonight. *They can use the canal or go home,* he thought.

He pressed his eye against a crack in the wooden door to see candlelight filtering through the second-floor shutters of the hatmaker's house. Geertruid and Joos were still awake.

The moon, high over head, turned the street into a patchwork of light and shadow. Before long, staring through the narrow crack made Jason's vision blur, and the buildings across the street began to waver. He knuckled his eyes, but his focus didn't improve.

The light in the upstairs window still flickered.

Jason couldn't keep Cat out of his mind. By now her arms and legs must be stiff, maybe tingly, from lack of movement. And her head probably ached from the chest's stuffy interior.

Shortly after nine, the tavern emptied out, each man swinging a lantern as he headed home. There was no singing now, only staggering.

An hour later, the upstairs window went black. Bedtime. Finally. The waiting was even worse now, each minute a big piece of forever. What was Cat doing? Jason's foot tapped staccato rhythms against the dirt floor. Where was she? His patience gave out, and he unbolted the outhouse door, ready to invade the hatmaker's house. Then he saw her. With wraithlike grace, Cat glided out of the passageway and stood on the street. Jason burst from the outhouse and threw his arms around her.

"I have it," she whispered, freeing an arm from his embrace to hold up the list.

Jason slid his finger down the crumpled parchment, counting eleven names.

"I must read the names," Cat whispered. She squinted and so did Jason, but the moon, bright as it was, didn't give enough light to decipher the signatures, some cramped, others scrawled.

"We can't destroy it until I read it. I need to know every one of Papa's friends who helped him—and the Beggars' cause.

"I'll keep it safe," he offered.

"Good." Cat watched while Jason lifted his tunic to tuck the list into the top of his shorts.

"I heard you upstairs," she said, gratitude ringing clear in her voice. "I heard you with Joos and Geertruid. You saved me. I would have taken those squeaky front stairs if you hadn't warned me." Then her nose twitched. "Is *that* where you've been waiting?" she asked, pointing toward the outhouse.

Jason could see she was laughing without a sound. Then she looked down the street, and her mirth died.

Chapter Thirty

Cat touched Jason's arm, beckoning him back to the safety of the passageway.

"Down there," she whispered.

Jason peered over her shoulder to see the crier at the end of the street. The man ambled toward them, his lantern swinging in arcs of light at his side. Every few steps, he broke the pendulum pattern to hold the lantern aloft, letting it shine like a distant lighthouse.

"All's well" came his cry. His footfalls couldn't be heard because he was too far away, but his words cut into the night.

Cat and Jason huddled in the passageway where the darkness cloaked them and the crier's lantern beams wouldn't reach them.

"He'll pass by. Then we'll go," she whispered while Jason fidgeted behind her.

For more than a minute, they waited and watched as the lantern swung to and fro. Then Cat reached back and dug her nails into Jason's arm.

He, too, had heard footsteps on the back stairs.

In the next second, Geertruid's voice thundered. "I know there was someone in the kitchen!"

"Just the cat, my love, just the cat," Joos said.

As they argued, their voices rose, but their footsteps seemed to stop.

"No! I always bolt the kitchen door after supper, and now it's unbolted. I suppose you think the cat did that!"

"But my pet, you've forgotten to bolt the back door before. Besides, there's no one in the kitchen now."

Geertruid snorted. "Don't be stupid. Of course there's no one in the kitchen *now*. The culprit escaped down the back stairs and into the passageway. If you hadn't taken so long lighting the candle, we'd have caught him. Look in the passageway."

Jason heard Joos shuffling down the back stairs. There was a thud.

"I think he bumped into the chicken coop," Cat whispered.

Jason took Cat's hand, and they crept out of the passageway to steal softly along the front of the smithy's house, in and out of shadows sketched by a luminous moon. As they tiptoed along, they tucked the hems of their tunics into their rope belts to free their legs for flight. Jason kicked off his cumbersome clogs.

For a moment, they crouched behind the smithy's wagon and looked back. The crier reached the hatmaker's house just as Joos came to the end of the passageway. Poor dithering Joos. His candle, touched by a breath of breeze, wavered and went out.

"Who goes there?" The crier's words burst like musket fire, and he aimed his light toward the passageway.

Joos was caught—without a lantern.

Geertruid appeared next to her husband. "Fools, both of you. A thief was in my kitchen, and now he's escaping. Get after him!"

Even the night crier bowed to Geertruid's authority. He held his lantern high, straining to see the neighboring buildings. Geertruid gave him a shove toward the blacksmith's property.

"There!" she screeched, pointing at Cat and Jason. "I see two of them. Thieves! Thi-eee-ves!"

The moon moved from behind a cloud, and Jason and Cat were now sprinkled with light. They started to run.

"Thieves! Wake up! Thieves," the crier shouted, setting off a hue and cry.

Almost instantly, a man's tousled head showed in a window above the fleeing pair. "Here they are!" he cried. "Thieves!"

The cry was taken up in the next house, and the next, and the next. One by one, two by two, townspeople in nightshirts hastened onto the street and took up the pursuit.

Cat and Jason ran in frantic flight. They fled down the street, past houses and shops and the big Catholic church. They ducked into an alley on their right, which brought them to the next street over. Without slackening their pace, they veered left and ran until a house loomed straight ahead: a dead end. Behind them, their pursuers burst from the alley and spread across the street, blocking the retreat route.

"We're trapped." Cat could barely breathe.

"No." Jason took her hand and led her into a corridor between two wooden houses. It was so narrow they could barely fit single file. Only a sliver of moonlight showed the way. They emerged onto a well-worn path that twisted and turned, taking them behind more houses, past sheds, around pig pens and chicken coops.

The clamor of their followers grew fainter, and Jason envisioned them squeezing into the corridor, a rushing flow of pursuers thinning to a trickle of bunglers who bumped into each other's backs, hit noses on shoulders, stubbed toes on heels.

Jason now saw no one behind them; they had gained ground.

"Rest a second." He knew Cat was tiring, and the burn on her leg must be hurting. They needed somewhere to hide, a safe place until the hunt died down. Jason tried to get his bearings. Nothing looked familiar. Their path butted into another alley, and Jason sniffed the air. "The smell. It's familiar."

"It's you," Cat said.

"No. It's more than me."

In the distance, he detected the slap of shoes on dirt. The chase was still on.

"This way." He grasped Cat's hand. "I know where we are. I stayed clear of this alley when I came to town."

After a dozen steps, Cat balked, shaking her head. "No."

But Jason dragged her with him. "Yes," he whispered, well aware of the stench and gore that would surround them in tanner's alley. That trade was far from pretty—neither was it sweetly perfumed. Turning animal skins into leather for shoes and scabbards, bellows and bagpipes took an extra-strong stomach. No wonder townspeople never wanted to go near tanner's alley.

So, who's going to look for us there? Jason thought.

Chapter Thirty-One

Cat was bent over, and Jason held her forehead as she retched, silently but uncontrollably.

"Sorry," she said when her heaving stopped.

"No problem." Jason was surprised that his own stomach wasn't turning inside out from the blood and gore around them. They stood amid a collection of low-roofed, open-sided structures that housed the tannery.

Cat touched Jason's shoulder. "You still have the list, don't you?"

"No, not anymore."

He heard her suck in air.

"I ate it," he said.

"You what?"

"I ate it. I was afraid we'd get caught by the crier. In the passageway, while you were watching him, I tore the parchment into bits. Then I stuffed them down." Jason smacked his lips and grinned.

He could see the shine of tears in Cat's eyes as she started to laugh. "Tasty supper?"

"The best. Needed a bit of mustard, though." Then he hesitated before going on. "I'm sorry, Cat. I know you wanted to read the names, but . . ."

"No," she interrupted, gently placing her hand over his mouth. "You were right. I was wrong. We should never have risked carrying that list, even for a minute. As long as it's gone . . . thank you, Jason."

Cat said no more because the sound of voices came from the alley.

"We need cover." Jason hoped the nauseous smells would keep their pursuers out of the tannery, but he couldn't count on it.

He and Cat stepped gingerly around the work area. A single hide, brown and smooth, hung over a ladder ready for the bootmaker. The rest of the skins were still raw, many covered with hair and flesh, all in various stages of the tanning process. Some were piled in heaps, others were stretched out on the ground, and still others were draped over log beams. There were also vats of foul-smelling liquid and mounds of what looked like dog dung.

Nowhere in all the tanner's trappings did they see a suitable place to hide.

A voice, loud and strident, cut through the night. It was Geertruid's, no mistake about that. "They came this way. I know they did." Behind her, the alley was alive with glowing lanterns.

"This way." Jason hustled Cat to a waist-high stack of skins. He guessed they were ox or cow, but it didn't matter because they were as broad as tablecloths and would cover the two of them if he drew up his legs. Jason threw back the top skin. Maggots. With several swipes, he cleared them away while flies buzzed into the air. The exposed underside of the skin was damp and fleshy, and the smell reminded Jason of fish rotting on a Chicago beach.

He motioned to Cat. She cringed but climbed onto the stack and lay facedown. Jason squeezed in beside her, pulling the top skin over them. He trusted that it was bulky enough to conceal their body contours.

A minute ticked by, and they didn't move. It was enough just to breathe, to stay alive. Then Jason heard Geertruid squawking above the mutterings of the mob. "I'm sure they're hiding in there. It's the only place they could be."

Someone, not Joos, took up the verbal battle. "Nobody would hide in there! And I don't intend to set one foot on the tanner's property. Not tonight, nor tomorrow, nor ever. I'd carry that stink to my grave."

"Amen to that," said another. More male voices chorused agreement.

"My Joos will go in," Geertruid announced. "He's not squeamish, are you, Joos?"

Jason heard no reply from the hatmaker.

"If you're going in there, take my lantern," someone offered.

"Thank you," Geertruid said. "Now, Joos, walk around. Look under that wooden beam. No, not there. The beam with the goatskin over it. Yes, there. What do you see?"

Again, Jason heard no answer from Joos.

"Take your hand away from your mouth, Joos," Geertruid ordered. "I can't understand you if you're holding your nose."

"I don't see anything, dearest."

"You're not really looking. Stop pussyfooting around. What about the vats?"

Jason could feel Cat trembling next to him as the hatmaker's footsteps moved toward the liquid baths, not far from their hiding place.

"Try that stack of skins instead," Geertruid said.

Joos's footsteps came closer.

"Look under them," she ordered.

"But dearest, they're so smelly. And there's blood on them."

"Joooos!"

Jason prayed that the hatmaker for once would refuse to do Geertruid's bidding. He didn't.

Both Jason and Cat stayed dead still as Joos touched the top skin. A corner of it rose an inch, and Jason could see the hatmaker's fat fingers in the lantern light.

Then Joos stopped. Bells had begun to clang, their tenor notes pounding the air for everyone's attention.

"Fire!"

Joos dropped the corner of the skin, and Jason and Cat lay in darkness until the sounds of the mob died away. When Jason finally peeked out, they were alone. But the peal of bells still tore up the night.

He threw back the skin and climbed down. "What happened?"

"The tower bells are signaling a fire, and every household has to send a firefighter. Fires happen often. One spark on a thatched roof could burn down the whole town."

Jason thought of the timber houses, standing shoulder to shoulder with roofs of wooden shingles or thatch; too few had been made of tile. "I'd run, too, if I thought my house was on fire."

"They'll be fined if they don't get home," Cat said. "Everyone has to bring a leather bucket too. Doesn't your town do this?"

"No," said Jason, remembering red fire engines and ambulances and cop cars. "Sometime I'll tell you what we do."

While the bells still tolled, they left the tanner's and made their way through paths and back alleys to the hatmaker's street. From here, Jason could easily find his way to the canal bridge and the field beyond.

But this street was now packed with people, all in a frenzy, fighting the fire that roared its way from house to house.

The hatmaker's home was still untouched. "I hope Joos's house doesn't burn," Cat said.

Jason faced her, startled.

"I know," she said, "Joos turned me over to the bailiff. Maybe it's just because the house once belonged to Papa. I don't know."

Jason thought he understood. And he knew for sure that the art shop with Bruegel's snow scene would survive the flames.

He glanced at Cat's tunic. It was smeared with blood. So was his. And they both smelled like a death pit. "I don't think we'll make it down the street looking like this, even if we carry a bucket."

"We won't," she said. "Someone will catch us. I don't know which is worse, the sight of us or the smell of us."

Jason struggled to draw a mental map. It was the canal's route he needed to recall. His thoughts went back to days ago when the children had pulled him across the canal bridge. He remembered that the waterway ran along the outskirts of town, right past the playground and the fields beyond.

"Over there." At a run, Jason guided Cat across the street, trying his best to steer around any frantic firefighters who might detect their smell or see their bloody clothes. The two now stood beside the outhouse where Jason had hidden earlier in the night.

"You told me you can swim," he said.

Cat looked down at the canal and then back at Jason. "In there?"

"In there."

She grabbed at her tunic. "In these? They'll pull us down. And they'll attract every predator in the forest that has a nose."

Without hesitation, Jason stripped to his shorts. Cat discarded her tunic and once again, was clad in only her woolen shift and soft-soled shoes, the bandage still bound about her leg.

Together, the two plunged into the canal's frigid water and began stroking through the filth, side by side.

Chapter Thirty-Two

Jason plunged into the pond, rinsing away the canal's filth. The water was cold, and moonbeams danced on its surface. Charles splashed beside him. How long had it been since he first bathed here? A week? Almost.

He now knew which grass to grab for a washcloth, and with soap from Cat's pack, he scrubbed away all remnants of the day: the sweat, the dust of the hovel, the stench of the canal, the blood of the tannery. Dunking and shivering, he looked over at Cat. She was already clean and perched demurely on the bank, dressed in her bodice, skirt, and still-damp shoes and shift. Her hair, drying into tight curls, was encircled with the green ribbon.

"All right," Jason said. "I'm getting out."

Cat retreated to the bushes while Jason climbed from the pond. He wrung out his shorts, then flapped them in the air, hoping they'd dry. They didn't. He pulled them on anyway and retrieved his clothes from their hiding place in the tree. In seconds, he was dressed.

"Ready," he said, feeling better than if he'd visited a spa.

Cat left the bushes and came close to run her hand over Jason's bristly chin. "Hmmm."

"Well, it was you who forgot to pack the shaving knife," he teased. "What can I do?"

"I like a beard," she said, "when the right person wears it." Jason could have sworn she was flirting.

Hand in hand, they walked toward the town with Charles frisking beside them. Cat found a cluster of hazel shrubs within sight of the children's playground. There, they waited, sitting on the ground with Charles stretched out beside them. Jason put his arm around Cat.

He didn't want to arrive at the house of Griet's brother in the dark morning hours. Dawn was a better time. Then alone, he'd go to the place of the mud pies. If he got back to Chicago, Jason knew he'd miss Cat, but those feelings would fade when he saw Karen. He was sure of that.

As their last few hours together passed swiftly by, the red of the town fire drained slowly from the sky. "You'll be all right in Paris?" Jason asked. "What will you do?"

"Griet's sister will look after me. And Paris is a marvelous city." She pulled up blades of grass and threw them in the air so they showered down on Jason. "I'll become a weaver. I'm very good at it.

"Papa's weavers taught me everything. I told you that. I can wash fleece, comb it, and spin it into yarn," she said, twirling two fingers in the air to make dozens of invisible circles. "I can dye yarn, too, and weave it into cloth to your liking. I make wonderful designs—right out of my head." She was laughing now, and Jason knew she was trying to allay his fears about her future. She opened her red-blanket bundle.

"You wove that, didn't you?"

"Yes," she said proudly. "On the hermit's little loom. I even found some madder root he had stored, so I was able to dye the yarn red."

She rummaged through the bundle and pulled out their last chunk of bread. After dividing it into three pieces, she handed the biggest one to Jason. He refused it, taking the smallest.

"I'll have lots to eat when I get home," he said. Pizza and burgers and fries with ketchup—if he got there.

Charles woke just long enough to gulp his share, then sank back into his easy slumber.

"Will you study law?" Cat asked.

Jason didn't need to think even a moment before answering. "No. I won't. I'll study, but I'll study art and learn to design."

"I'm glad you decided that." She pulled from her bodice the folded-up sketch that Jason had done at the gallows.

"You don't still have that crazy thing!"

"I do. And it'll remind me that someday you'll be a wonderful artist in your century." Cat didn't look at him when she asked, "Would I like your century?"

Jason gave no answer as his thoughts went into madhouse mode. He imagined himself introducing Cat to his parents and Karen. "Hi, Mom, Dad, Karen," he'd say. "I'd like you to meet Catherine Juliana Eijngaard. She's from Belgium or somewhere around there. She just got to the U.S. We met at an outdoor party. It was a wild blast, and everyone was drunk, but we were sober, so we kind of hung together. And then we sort of got married. Not really, just a mock kind of ceremony." Then he'd add, "But we can have it annulled, just to make sure." His mom's mouth would drop open. His dad would shout, "What the hell is going on here?" And Karen would get hysterical. Then she'd size up Cat's outfit and say, "Is *that* the new look from Europe?"

Cat frowned. "What are you thinking, Jason?"

He waved away her question.

She asked nothing more about his thoughts or his century. Instead, she talked about the times she visited England with her father. "We went often. Papa used to buy this wonderful wool there. It comes from long-haired sheep that roam the fens and grasslands. They're special sheep." Happy and harmless, her chatter presented no challenges to Jason.

In the distance, a rooster crowed although the sun had not yet sparked a dawn in the eastern sky. Cat stood up. "It's time."

"Yes." He took her hand and they walked slowly. Behind them, the fields were empty, and there was almost no sign of life at the town's edge. Gradually, the sun touched the horizon with a delicate pink.

As they walked, Jason stole long glances at Cat, acutely aware of a gnawing in his stomach that wasn't from hunger or the tension of trying to get home. He said nothing, memorizing every detail of her face.

Sooner than Jason wanted, they passed by the canal bridge and came to where Griet's brother lived. "Let me tell Griet I'm not going to Paris with you."

Cat shook her head. "You've shown me where Griet is staying, and I promise to come back here later. But right now, I'm going with you to the playground."

Jason grabbed Cat's shoulders. "We decided I'd see you safely to Griet. Then, and only then, would I go home."

"You decided. I didn't," she said.

"I need to know you're safely with Griet," he argued.

"Jason! Listen to me." Cat stepped back, and her hands were now on her skinny hips, her chin jutting outward in defiance. "You've told me this wild tale about your century. Maybe it's true, and maybe it isn't. I want to know. And if you stand in that mud for very long and go nowhere, I'll slap you and drag you to Paris with me." She tried to laugh.

Jason argued no more. He knew he'd feel the same if their roles were reversed.

They began to retrace their steps. There was so much to say, yet they said nothing.

Halfway there, doubts shivered through Jason. What if he did wait in the mud and nothing happened? He couldn't face such a fate. He hated this century.

When they finally came to the playground, they stood together, quietly, holding hands. Then Jason took off his ring. "If I leave here, I want you to have this. Maybe the weaving business won't be so good in Paris. You can always sell it for money."

"No. That's your ring. You might want to give it to Karen someday—if you get home."

"Please, Cat. I want you to have it, no matter where I am."

She tilted her head and smiled, just a little. She took the ring. "I'll never sell it. You know that."

Jason put his arms around her. They held each other for only a moment before she backed away and sat down with Charles to watch and wait.

Jason studied the mud near where the children had stacked their pies. He walked to the center of it and stood motionless. He thought of his parents, of home.

Nothing happened.

He thought of Karen.

Nothing happened.

He looked at Cat. She didn't speak, and her expression didn't change. She just waited. Try as he might, Jason couldn't get his thoughts together while he watched her. He turned his back and closed his eyes.

He thought about the gallery and the paintings and the marble bench, and he concentrated harder than he had ever concentrated before.

Chapter Thirty-Three

Jason shook his head, then pressed his fingertips against his temples, just to make sure he was seeing straight. He also patted the seat beneath him. It was hard. And marble.

Yes, he was back in the gallery.

All the fears of the past week—fear for Cat's safety, fear for his own life, fear that he'd never get home—thrashed around inside him. For a time he sat unmoving until a laugh burst out of him. He was home! What explanation could he possibly give his mom and dad and Karen and everyone else who had been searching for him? The truth wouldn't cut it— they'd think he was insane. He'd have to make up something. But first he needed to find out exactly how long he'd been missing. A week? That sounded right, but he wanted to be sure.

He approached the museum guard in the adjacent gallery. "Can you tell me what day it is?"

"Tuesday." The guard looked bored, like this was his millionth question of the day.

"And the date?"

"May Day. May first."

May first? He had lived through all those trials in the sixteenth century, yet no time had elapsed here. He couldn't understand—nor did he try.

"What time is it?" he asked.

"Four o'clock." The guard folded his arms across his chest. "Hey, kid, you want to know about the museum, I'll tell ya. But I'm not a walking calendar, or wristwatch, either."

Four o'clock on Tuesday, May 1. He wouldn't have to explain anything to anyone. No one would have missed him. Impulsively, he grabbed the guard's hand and shook it, then ran out of the gallery.

He rushed down the steps and pushed through the revolving doors. Karen would never know he had gone anywhere!

With a half hour to spare, Jason decided to skip the bus and walk up Michigan Avenue. He wanted to hug everyone. There were office workers with briefcases, tourists with cameras, children with balloons, and homeless people with their plastic bundles, all jostling by and around each other on the sidewalk. Traffic crawled. When he reached the bridge over the Chicago River, he stopped to watch a sightseeing boat chug its way toward Lake Michigan. At the Tribune Tower, he stopped again, this time to touch the rocks from faraway places that had been cemented into the building's facade. It was great to be back.

He decided to pick up his pace so he wouldn't be late. But he was. Karen was already standing outside Rosa's pizzeria. Her sweater, which clung slightly, was the exact blue of her eyes, and her lips were lightly glossed. She looked gorgeous, and Jason could feel a thrill kindling inside him.

"Hi," he said and smiled.

"You're late. And look at you!" A frown turned Karen's features from soft to hard. "You need a shave, for heaven's sake. And your clothes are all rumpled." Her glance took in every inch of him. "Look at the mud on your shoes. And where are your socks?"

Considering what he'd been through, Jason thought he looked terrific. He started to laugh.

Karen didn't share his amusement. "Where *are* your socks?"

"They got wet in the rain, so I took them off," he fibbed.

She grimaced as if dealing with a naughty two year old and marched into the restaurant ahead of him. The place was packed, so they had to wait.

"If you had been on time, we'd already have a booth," she said. "Now, we won't get to Saks until after seven. You know how long it takes to get waited on here when it's crowded."

Jason didn't react.

Standing nearly a head taller than Karen, he looked down on her black hair. It glistened with highlights, like sun rays in a midnight sky. Jason had never minded that the highlights came out of a bottle at Pierre's salon. But now, he wondered why she bothered.

She tugged Jason's shoulder downward and stood on tiptoe, her voice soft as though she had a secret to share. "You should have seen what Muriel wore today! Straight out of a rag bag. And she had the nerve to say her mother bought the dress in New York."

"Hmmm," Jason replied. He breathed deeply, savoring the aroma of the pizza. "I'm starved."

"You had lunch. You can't be that hungry."

By the time they were seated, Jason was ready to eat the checkered tablecloth. When their antipasto finally came, he dove into it while Karen nibbled.

"I can't wait to get to Saks," she said. "There's this incredible dress. I hope they still have a size six. I could wear it Saturday night."

"Saturday night?"

"The spring dance! Eddie Bishop asked me, too, but naturally I'm going with you."

"Yes. Yes. Good," he said, shoving a piece of pizza into his mouth. Eddie Bishop was a big something or other on the football team. Jason couldn't remember exactly what.

"Of course, if you'd rather I went with Eddie, just say so."

"Oh, Karen, stop playing games. You know I want to take you."

She smiled at her little victory.

Jason continued to stuff his face while Karen's conversation dwelled on the dress at Saks, summer sandals at Lord & Taylor, and dance decorations that were to feature real roses.

"Jason, you're not listening."

"I am. I am," he said, for the first time realizing how little he had actually heard of Karen's monologues. If his life depended upon it, he couldn't recount even half of what she'd said in the last fifteen minutes. He knew, though, that there had been no laughter.

"What's the matter with you?" she said. "You're so different tonight."

She was absolutely correct. He was very different from the Jason he used to be.

"Finish your pizza. We need to hurry. I want to try on the dress." Karen looked at her watch. "It's already seven."

"Ready," Jason said, stopping himself before adding the hatmaker's, "dearest".

When the waiter brought the check, Jason pulled out his wallet and opened it. A strip of dirty cloth and two crushed violets fell onto the table.

Karen stared. "What is that?"

He picked up the violets and carefully rewrapped them in the cloth. He looked into Karen's eyes, past the mascara lashes and into the thoughts beyond. He knew that he didn't want to go shopping with her now—or ever again. And he knew that he didn't want to go through the rest of his life without Cat. "I can't go with you," he said. "I left something at the Art Institute."

"So what?" Karen snapped. "I suggest you come with me, or you just might find yourself without a date for Saturday's dance."

"Maybe you better call Eddie." Jason got up, counted out money for the bill and tip, and dropped it by his plate.

Karen's words followed him: "You'll be very sorry for this, Jason Becker!"

He walked out.

On Michigan Avenue, he hopped on a southbound bus almost immediately.

Cat might well be on her way to Paris by now, but he'd follow her—and find her. He was scared, though, afraid something might have gone wrong, preventing her from leaving. Maybe Alba had grabbed her before she could get out of town.

He was still on north Michigan Avenue when the bus slowed to a stop in snarled traffic. They sat. Ten minutes went by, and still the bus didn't move. Jason checked his watch for the tenth time: 7:30. He had only a half hour before the Art Institute closed.

He made his way through the crowded aisle to the front of the bus. "What's up ahead?" he asked the driver.

"Looks like an accident on the bridge. We'll just have to wait it out." The driver pulled out a sandwich and popped the top of a soda can.

Jason heard sirens coming down Michigan. "I want off," he said and pushed through the bus door.

He walked, then ran. At the bridge, people were clustered at the accident scene, but Jason kept running, without even a glance toward the disaster.

By the time he went through the doors of the Art Institute, he was out of breath. He fumbled in his wallet to find his family membership card. He flashed it at the guard who took tickets.

"You only got seven minutes," the guard said. "We can't let you upstairs now."

"Please. I left something. I've got to get it. Please?"

The guard waved him on. "Make it fast."

Jason bounded up the stairs and took his place on the marble bench, annoyed that three viewers lingered in the gallery. They chatted and looked and chatted more. Then they strolled to the exit. At last, Jason sat alone.

He shut out all thoughts of his own place and time, staring at the painting, willing himself into the playground. A minute passed and nothing happened. It occurred to him that his trip to the sixteenth century might have been a one-shot adventure.

With every fiber of his being, he concentrated on the children and their games, blocking out all other thoughts. Again, nothing happened. Another minute went by. And another. Then, the gentlest of breezes blew through his hair, and the scent of salt air filled his nostrils. He could sense his surroundings dissolving.

And he was there.

He found Cat still sitting on the ground with Charles beside her. Her face was buried in her hands.

Jason called her name. When she looked up, he could see she had been crying. Around her neck was the green ribbon, and from it dangled his ring.

Her eyes were wide, and she let out the smallest of gasps. "Oh, I was hoping you'd come back. I waited for you, Jason."

"Cat, come with me. My century needs weavers. And you'll be safe from Alba."

She didn't move, except for her eyebrows, which arched.

"You'll like my century. I know you will. I'll show you a Bruegel painting, and I'll buy you an ice cream sundae. Come on, Cat."

Still, she didn't get up.

"Cat," he called again. "I want you to be with me. In my century, or any century." He held out his hand.

She smiled and ran to him with Charles bounding behind her. Jason pulled her close. Then, with the dog squeezed between them, they left the sixteenth century behind.

Endnote

With brush and paint, Pieter Bruegel(ca. 1525/1530–1569) gave us a glimpse of what rural life was like in sixteenth-century Flanders, which today is a region in northern Belgium.

Unlike many artists of his time, Bruegel shunned painting angels and heroes and wealthy people dressed in finery. Instead, he generally chose to capture the common people, unposed and clad in everyday clothes. In his paintings, workers plant gardens, harvest grain, rake hay, and herd cows. They steal honey from bees and hunt with dogs on a cold snowy day. They seldom smile, even when they're dancing in the street or feasting at a wedding.

Bruegel lived in harsh times. People suffered under the heel of the ruling Spanish. They also endured recurrences of the plague and periods of starvation caused by crop failures and extreme winters. The grimness of these days is vividly portrayed in the artist's paintings of blind men stumbling, cripples begging, and a gallows ready for the next hanging.

At the time Bruegel painted, Spain's King Philip II reigned over the Netherlands, which then included Flanders. Philip was a staunch Catholic who ruled from afar, had no understanding of his subjects or their culture, and couldn't speak their languages. Even worse, he hated the Protestant religions that were spreading throughout the Netherlands. And he had no qualms about killing heretics, a name given to people who didn't follow the teachings of the Catholic Church.

Spain's religious persecution infuriated local nobles. In desperation, they petitioned the Spanish government to be more tolerant. But their pleas went unheeded. They were dismissed with empty promises and derisively called a bunch of beggars. From then on, these dissenting nobles—and later their followers—operated under the name "Beggars."

Annoyed by the nobles' protests, Philip sent the ruthless Duke of Alba with an army to the Netherlands to root out heresy, punish rebels, confiscate lands, and restore order. Alba arrived in August 1567, nearly a year before the fictional story of Jason and Cat takes place. In no time at all, Alba and his infamous Council of Blood had accused approximately 12,000 persons. A thousand or more were executed. Fear lived everywhere.

Imagine you are transported, like Jason, into this bygone world of Bruegel. More than likely, your parents are peasants, so your life isn't easy.

You share a thatched-roof cottage in the country with your mother and father, your sisters and brothers. Sometimes a pig wanders in, too. At first light, you're up, and you rush to your baby sister because it's your job to keep rats out of her cradle. She's fine, and you breathe easier.

Like your parents and older siblings, you follow the custom of eating just twice daily, at midday and dusk. Only young children break their fast in the morning with a chunk of bread.

School? Not for you. Your parents need you to work. Besides, there are no public schools. Education rests mainly in the hands of tutors and the churches, both Catholic and Protestant. But the current oppression and unrest have disrupted even this education.

All day you toil beside your family in the fields of a wealthy landowner. Luckily, there's a break at noon when you sit in the shade and eat dark bread made more tasty with cheese, onions, and salt. At day's end you return to the cottage where more work awaits you. You help to tend the family's garden, chickens, two pigs, and a goat. Bedtime arrives shortly after supper. Candles are costly, and you prefer sleeping to sitting in the dark.

You've heard of Antwerp, but you'll probably never go there, even though it's only 40 miles (64 kilometers) away. What a pity because the city is one of Europe's largest centers of trade and banking. Fun times for you center closer to home: walking to market and celebrating feast days with your family. You look forward to hangings, too, because your friends will be there.

Do you know about Bruegel and his paintings? Probably not. Eeking out a living leaves little time for art. Do you know about Alba and his Council of Blood? Probably so. Frightening news spreads quickly.

Do you wonder what you might have looked like if you had lived back then? Go to your library and check out a book on Pieter Bruegel. You'll see.